MANUEL SANTOS VARELA

HORUS

Translation: Sarah Marshall

Copyright

© 2014. 2016. Text and covers: Manuel Santos Varela.
© 2016. Translation: Sarah Marshall.
Novel registered with safecreative.org.
    Registration number:
    Spanish edition: 1404230643164.
    English edition: 1607028289005.
ISBN: 978-1535071123.
Legal deposit: Z 478-2016.
All rights reserved.

Cover photograph:
Inside the temple of Abu Simbel.
David Roberts (Edinburgh, 1796 – London, 1864)
Public domain.

Index

A dedication

A word

Day 1 9

Day 2 81

Day 3 151

Day 4 177

A note of thanks

A last thing

A dedication

For María Victoria, the person who most puts up with my "autistic moments of creative concentration".

A word

The novel HORUS is a good example of this clinical case of what I have just christened "autistic moments of creative concentration". It delighted me to submit it for the "2012 UPC Short Science Fiction Novel Award" because, idiot that I am, I thought they still published an annual compilation of the three or four best entries. So, in order to finish writing it on time, I spent December 2011 holed up in my mental submarine, several feet below the everyday sea swell, with no radio contact.

When I went (in very good company, by the way) to the prize ceremony in June 2012, the first thing Miquel Barceló said to me was, "You do know that the Ediciones B agreement no longer exists, don't you?"

No, I didn't know that. That is what comes of submerging oneself so deeply. Returning to the surface, I put a swift end to the problem by formatting the book and dsigning the cover myself. Thus, thanks to Amazon, which doesn't impose any condition other than respecting its formats, all fans of science fiction can judge whether so many hours of immersion were worth their while. Or not.

Regardless of whether the verdict is favourable or damning, thank you in advance.

Day 1

Friday, 3 May 2030

"Health, Lord of divine words. You who preside over the mysteries of the heavens and the earth, great god of primordial times. You, the originator, who provided the magic formulas, who provided the writing that makes houses prosper by giving them a good foundation. You, who shows each god his place and each profession its statute, keep each house, each field, each country within its just limits."

Hymn to Tehouti, lord of hieroglyphics.
Back of a statue found in tomb 192, Thebes.
Currently in the Neues Museum in Berlin.

HORUS

1

Department of Molecular Genetics
Glasgow University
Local Time: 13:30

Doctor Ted Howard is seated in front of the television. As is his custom on Fridays at this hour, he has just eaten a double-decker sandwich washed down with an alcohol-free beer while he half watches the headlines on the news channel. The television, a flexible model three millimetres thick with very low power consumption, is temporarily stuck to the wall. Although it is on at a reasonable volume, Doctor Howard neither sees the images nor hears the sound. He is as still as the Great Sphinx of Giza; unblinking in an immobile posture, he hardly even seems to be breathing.

The news item has caught him by surprise and he cannot fully assimilate it. That bloody pig. That disgusting swine. That tricky bastard. Doctor Kasigi.

Ted once saw him in person at a convention; he couldn't recall which year. The best geneticists had gathered for three days in Oslo, ostensibly to hear the presentations generously offered by others for the purpose of sharing knowledge. In reality, it was to spy on one another, to keep the others at bay by spouting false clues in order to create the greatest delay possible in their rivals' work. In the second session of the second day, Doctor Kasigi deliberately bored the audience with a soporific two-hour speech on the most widely known and unproductive aspects of statistical analysis applied to bacterial genetics. A smooth-shaven, slim man of exquisite manners, in his chest beat a heart of stone well below freezing point.

That good-for-nothing swindler, Doctor Kasigi Hiroshi. His assistants sometimes called him Hiroshi-san, Hiroshi-sensei or something similar. The suffix "san" is used to show respect and admiration. As if using "doctor" weren't enough. Respect and admiration for such a miserable man. Hundreds of people working fourteen-hour days so that this guy could take all the credit. He is the head of the team so it might seem logical that every living creature would congratulate him. Perhaps it would be less painful had he ever uttered a single syllable of acknowledgement to his assistants, to his forerunners or to Doctor Iritani, who had left the work nearly completed before retiring. Life is so unfair! Everyone thought he had achieved it by himself, working alone in a basement with no help, no financial support, with nothing more than his own patience and courage, as if he were the reincarnation of Mendel.

Where is the justice, for Christ's sake? If anyone dares to compare him with Mendel, I'll rip their tongue out.

What really bothers you is that you're second again. Admit it. Admit it once and for all and drink a real beer to celebrate instead of this yellow-coloured soda water. Second place. As always. Yep, that's me, always coming second. Even at birth I came second. Always second. Then there was that bloody skating race. Second again. Always second.

"Is it true that you were second-in-line for your promotion, Doctor Howard?"

"Yes, it's true. Is that an important piece of information?"

I really thought the gold medal would have my name on it this time.

"A round of applause for Doctor Ted Howard. The man who managed to bring the Siberian mammoth back to life."

But, no. No, it wasn't me.

It was Kasigi. Doctor Kasigi. Doctor Kasigi Hiroshisan, better known as the "disgusting pig". Everybody thinking that he was working on sequencing bacteria.

"Here's to Doctor Kasigi. The man who has successfully cloned the woolly mammoth." A round of applause. What a bastard. He played us all.

The door opens and a woman runs in.

"Have you seen the news?" she shouts.

"Yes."

The young lady approaches Ted and kisses him on the cheek. They resemble one another closely, which is hardly surprising considering they are twins.

"Yes? That's it? That's all you have to say?" asks Nancy Howard.

"I don't what you else you want me to say," replies Ted.

"It's the news of the century!"

"I suppose so."

"You suppose? But you're not happy?" Ted's sister is mystified.

"Happy? Are you mad? Four years of my life just went down the drain and you want me to be happy?"

"Four years? What four years?"

"What do you mean 'What four years'? I've spent four years up to my eyeballs on this project. And now that bloody Japanese pig is going to get all the credit."

"What Japanese pig? The man who discovered the chamber is a Scot, just like us."

"What chamber?" Ted is utterly confused now.

"The burial chamber."

"What burial chamber?"

"They've found a burial chamber nobody knew existed. A huge chamber, forty metres below the Khafre pyramid. Khafre himself might be inside."

"Who cares?"

"I do. I'm an archaeologist, remember?"

"Have a good trip. Have fun digging up mummies."

"Yes, I will. Hey, what news were you talking about?"

"Doctor Kasigi has managed to clone the mammoth. One of his elephants has given birth to a live mammoth calf. They presented it to the press today."

"Kasigi... Isn't he the bacteria expert?"

"What does it matter now?"

"Och, get up and let your wee sister Nancy give you a cuddle."

Doctor Ted Howard rises with an air of weariness. He is a little taller than his sister. They hug and for a moment they look like a couple on a dance floor. A sweet couple experiencing the euphoria of the first term at university. They talk softly together, whispering like newlyweds. Both are very good looking, with a reddish hue to their hair and skin rude with health.

"When you were little and behaved yourself, you always asked for the same reward: 'I want to sleep with my sister'."

Ted kisses his sister on the neck, a slow, lingering kiss.

"Now I'm too old to ask you if we can sleep hand in hand. And you're even older than I am," he says.

"Yeah, not by much. Thirty minutes at most," Nancy protests.

"Thirty-four," Ted reminds her.

"Do you have any new projects on the go?" asks Nancy.

"No. Nothing."

"Then you can't stay here."

They pull apart and no longer seem like a couple dancing, but a couple arguing.

"What do you mean I can't stay here? I live here!"

"That's the problem. You live in the lab. You've stuck your life in a test tube."

"Hark who's talking: you've stuck your life in a sarcophagus. You live in a basement full of mummies. I win."

"You can't stay here. I'm dead serious. You'll spend

your time wallowing in self-pity because of that bloody mammoth experiment. He got there first. Move on."

"What are you, my psychiatrist?"

"I'm your big sister. I actually came here to say goodbye, but I like this change of plan better. Instead of saying bye, I'd rather we went together. Throw a few things in a bag, you're coming with me."

"Are you giving me orders?"

"You're coming with me, Ted."

"Where?"

"To my house for now, in bitter old London. In my jet car, we'll be there in less than ninety minutes. We can sleep at my place and then set off for Egypt first thing in the morning."

"No, thanks. I'm not going to Egypt, mummies give me the creeps."

"Nonsense! As if a mummy could hurt you."

"Tell that to Howard Carter and his friends. You know, the ones of the curse. The ones who opened Tutankhamun's tomb. Toast, the lot of them."

"Yeah, right, toast. You're forgetting the minor detail that Carter lived for another twenty years. Rather a slow curse."

"He stood on the threshold, watching while all the others went in to work. A very English attitude, by the way. All those who dared enter the mausoleum, who interrupted the pharaoh's rest, they all dropped dead. Struck down by the mummy's curse. Bothered that his wee three-thousand-year nap had been interrupted, he wanted to snooze a bit longer. Do you want us to fall victim to the dreaded curse of Khafre?"

"Are you sure that beer's alcohol free?"

"Positive."

"Well, you've short-circuited or something. You should get that looked at."

"How can I make you understand that I haven't lost anything in Egypt?"

"Are you sure?" Nancy moves closer to her brother, takes him by his wrists and wraps his arms around her waist. She hugs him around his neck. They seem like a couple on a dance floor once again. Standing on tiptoe, she nibbles his ear and murmurs softly, "So you don't want to have a holiday in Egypt with me, sharing a tent like when the two of us went camping on Jersey?"

"You need to get looked at as well."

"Who cares if you're my favourite lover?"

"Your boss, for instance? What's his name, that worthy man with the impeccable manners? Doctor or Reverend Mathias Shepard?

"He won't notice a thing."

"What? The typical absent-minded professor?"

"Worse. We're not embalmed, so we barely exist in his eyes."

"A mummy collector. Disgusting. I don't know if I want to meet him."

"Your pockets and your bedroom were disgusting. You spent your adolescence collecting strange bugs, brother dearest. Doctor's Shepard's jars of entrails will bring back fond memories."

"I didn't collect strange bugs, I collected morphologically notable arthropods."

"I was right, you see? 'Not just any intestine enters my collection, only the ones preserved in an optimum canopy.' You and the reverend will get on like a house on fire. You're two of a kind."

"Are we? Am I a worthy man with impeccable manners?"

"You were going to be a cloistered monk. You were saved from spending eternity in heaven, more bored than a tiger in a greengrocer's, because you had the great fortune of growing up with me by your side, and I took the trouble of perverting you a wee bit so you could come to hell, which is where the fun starts."

"Great, thanks a lot."

2

Aboard the Cargo Spaceship Antipodes
Time on the spacecraft: 14:15

"My dad was right all along! So right! 'Don't go into the scrap metal business,' he said. Don't go into the scrap metal business. So what do I do? Bang, I dive in headfirst. Scrap metal collector. 'But, Dad, don't you realise that everything's full of scrap metal? Easy work, Dad, easy work. Not much effort and a ton of dough.' 'You'll die of disgust and boredom.' And here I am. Yes sir, dying of disgust and boredom. My dad warned me! But, nooo, I had to dive right in." Nestor Sanchez, otherwise known as Drill, is in full flow as usual.

"You're getting on my last nerve, Drill," interjects Carlos Luis, whose nickname is Tripod.

"Oh, excuse me, my lord and master."

"Tripod is right, Drill. You're giving us all a headache with your griping. Give it a rest for a bit, won't you?" agrees Patch, whose real name nobody can remember.

"Give it a rest, give it a rest? I don't know how to be as lethargic as a crocodile! That's what you two are: two lazy crocodiles. Sitting there for hours, days, weeks, months on end! Especially Tripod, he's like a statue. He turns himself into stone. But I can't just lie down and count the flies. My dad was right all along! 'You'll get sick of waiting around. You're going to be bored to tears.' He warned me. But did I listen? Noooo, head first into the shit."

"There are no flies here, Drill," says Patch.

"I know there aren't. As much as I'd like there to be. I'd love to have a couple of dozen here right now, they'd give me more conversation than you guys do. This is worse than a game of Parcheesi with the colour blind."

"And my dad warned me. Don't play Parcheesi, Nestor, don't play Parcheesi," Tripod teases.

"That's right, take the mickey. Easy pickings. Take the mickey out of this poor guy who couldn't see the truth in his father's wise words, this stateless beggar who has nowhere to drop dead. But you know what? It's been a year. A whole year, you know? We've wasted a whole year of our lives in this damn quadrant and we won't earn a cent in premiums. We'll get paid the fucking minimum and given an 'If I've seen you, I don't remember'. Do you know what the hold looks like? Emptier than Chewbacca's head."

They hear the sound of the main hatch from the navigation room opening.

"Were you saying something about me, Mr Sanchez?"

"Nothing, Captain. Sorry if you heard me call you Chewbacca. Forgive me, Captain."

Captain William Tanner is a truly gigantic redheaded descendant of Irish parents and grandparents; the world heavyweight champion looks like a shrimp compared to him. He has to have all his clothes tailor-made and even freshly shaved he is hairier than a Siberian mammoth. As a boy he dreamt of becoming an astronaut. He wanted to land on unexplored planets and cover them on foot until they revealed all their treasures. As an adult he is captain of the cargo spaceship *Antipodes*, flight permit 23143Z, dedicated to searching for junk metal abandoned in space.

"It's just I'm getting antsy. The Chinese have taken all the sectors the regular flights pass through. They must be making a killing. Bolts, nuts, pressurized containers, springs... They say they even found an honest-to-goodness Technics welder once. What they must get paid, my God, just imagine. And us? Here in the fucking north-five gamma quadrant. Yeah, sure it sounds elegant and all. 'Go to the north-five gamma quadrant, sirs. Go and see what an empty vacuum it is, what spacious space, what a hollow cavity, what a clean hold you'll bring back and what shitty pay.'"

"And his father warned him," croons Patch.

"Leave my dad out of this, Patch. Don't make me madder. I guess it's my own fault for bringing him up all the time. I swear, Captain, they're going to have to tie me up and put a gag on me. I can't take it any more. How many dry days now, Aborigine?"

"Let me think," says Johnny Wash, a skinny, grizzly man covered in twisted tattoos and with a mop of such chaotic blond hair that it seems to have been combed by a blender. "Fourteen. It's been fourteen days without so much as a drawing pin."

John Walsh, known to all and sundry as Aborigine, is an imperturbable man born in the middle of the Australian desert. He has spent the past two hours sitting in front of the primary sensor, so he still has two more to go until he is relieved by one of the three currently off-duty crew members. For the past fortnight the screen has looked exactly the same: a green line endlessly revolving without a single blip in sight.

"We should never have accepted the job. Nobody's ever been here, not even a hologram. What do they expect us to find out here? Oh, that's right: a whole bunch of nothing. I was about to mention my dad again. Poor guy, spent his whole life swallowing dust, covered in grime at the bottom of the mine. Couldn't see he was the voice of experience. But, no, headed straight to north-five gamma quadrant. 'Go. Go see Mars. You'll see how pretty it is.' We should go home. That's all there is to it. We have to head home. Yeah, yeah, we're practically empty, but even if we stay here for the rest of the year and the next, we won't find anything to put in the hold."

"Stop exaggerating. We've picked up a ton of Siemens pieces. The trouble is that when the Germans set up a base, they lose less material than we do, that's the trouble," retorts Tripod.

"It doesn't matter. That's chump change. How long's it been since a mining probe came to Mars? Maybe everything's been picked up already. Captain, listen to what I'm saying, we have to go... Hey, what's the matter with Aborigine?"

Johnny Wash is looking at the sweeper on the tracker with his eyes bulging as if there were a camera connected to a lingerie catwalk and the signal was being sent to the screen.

"Holy shit!"

"What is it, Aborigine?"

"Come quick, Captain. Look at the screens."

On the main screen there is a green light blinking while on the secondary screen to the left hundreds of figures are running, all of which have marked a steady zero for the past fortnight. On the central secondary screen some axes and coordinates have appeared and on the right-hand secondary screen there are demarcations, relative velocities and directions. The identifier shows a blue light, the colour assigned to metal objects.

Everyone has crowded behind Aborigine, clutching the back of his seat.

"What the heck is that?"

"I don't know, Captain. But whatever it is, it's metal and it's big."

"Where did it come from?"

"No idea. I swear I didn't fall asleep. There was nothing there a second ago."

"Distance. Size. Direction."

"Don't rush me, Captain. The data is confusing. It seems to have come from outside the ecliptic. When it reached it, it aligned itself and now it's heading…"

"What do you mean it came from outside the ecliptic?" asks Tripod. "There's nothing outside the ecliptic."

"I don't know, guys. The computer is doing what it can with the signal."

"Do we have Doppler?" asks Captain Tanner.

"Look, it's recalibrating right now. Fuck, the Doppler is completely out of range."

"And what does that mean?" asks Drill, whose speciality is disassembling objects without stopping to identify what they are.

"I told you, it's enormous. And it appeared as fast as if it came out of a magician's hat. That's why it's out of range."

"And why we're calibrated to detect small stuff," Drill insists.

"I know. Don't try to tell me how to do my job. Let's see. Just a second. Holy mother of God. The computer says it's three hundred metres long."

"What? Three hundred metres? There's no way we've found a castoff that big," says Tripod incredulously.

"It's not a castoff. It's a whole ship."

"It'll be an empty fuel tank," conjectures the captain.

"A tank?" scoffs Drill. "A three-hundred-metre long fuel tank? How many spaceships have come this far with a liquid tank? That can't be right, Captain."

"What do you think, Aborigine?" asks Captain Tanner.

"It's a whole ship. And it's braking."

"Did you say it's braking? Are you high or something?" asks Tripod.

"Worse, I made a joint with one of your socks and smoked it. It's braking! And changing direction. It came from six three zero zero. The first reading showed almost five hundred thousand per hour. Now it's matching our speed and travelling with us at just under thirty thousand. Which means it has brakes a thousand times better than ours."

"The motherboard has melted," says Drill.

"Junk vessels don't go that fast or brake," Tripod comments.

"Or change direction," adds the captain.

"This one does, Captain. It entered the screen at more than seventy degrees above the ecliptic and it's crossed the two outer demarcations in three tenths of a second without bothering to correct the alignment with the eccentric path plotters. It's not out of position now. Now it's parallel to our zero point of origin."

"Speak English, Aborigine. No more jargon!"

"Its entry direction to the solar system wasn't on the same plane as the one the planets orbit on. It arrived at an almost perpendicular angle. But now it's moving on the planets' plane towards the inner planets."

"That's impossible," states Carlos Luis. "I wouldn't believe it even if I was soaked in bootleg whisky."

"Well, that's what the computer says, Tripod. Or at least that's what the telemeter says. The thermal sensors aren't detecting a thing."

"Why has it slowed down?" asks William Tanner.

"I guess because it's seen us."

"But you just said the thermal sensors aren't detecting anything. That means it's a dead ship."

"Or just a boulder," adds Tripod.

"It's metal, goddammit. Can't you see the blue plotter?"

"Or it's got an automatic thermal shield," says the captain.

"It's seen us? Is that what you said? He's out of his mind. Martians, man, and Aborigine says they've seen us. Amazing, my friends. If only my dad was here now. Bored to death, hey? Well, take that: head first into a space adventure. Hey, what if they attack us? We haven't even got water pistols on board."

"If they dare to come in here, Aborigine can asphyxiate them with his morning farts."

"Very funny, Tripod. Why don't you kill them with a swipe of your dick?"

"I have to look after it in case one of my girlfriends is waiting for my return."

"Quiet. That's enough nonsense. It can't be anything more than a tank," says the captain.

"So how's it changing direction?" asks Aborigine.

"It might have a leak from a hinge-shaped hole. When enough pressure accumulates, the hole opens and the ship moves backwards a little and turns. All that action and reaction shit."

"That doesn't add up, Captain. I'm telling you, it manoeuvred and aligned itself with the field zero."

"The telemeter circuits must be cooked, that's what's happened. How can it be an operative ship? We have to fix our own machines."

"Everything's green, can't you see?"

"I don't care about your green lights. We've short-circuited," insists Captain Tanner.

"It's manoeuvred. This is a trip!" Drill is pleased that something is finally happening.

"Let's see if they're really Martians and have come to do evil," says Tripod.

"You'll see. It's nothing more than a drifting tank. For now, shut down the communications and turn off the radio beacon."

"Communications shut down. Radio beacon off. Can I ask why, Captain?"

"I don't want anyone hovering. Whatever it is, we found it and we're going to divvy it up between ourselves. Even if we have to take it apart with a screwdriver."

"Here, here!" cheers Drill.

"Time until visual contact?" asks the captain.

"I don't know, a few hours. Three or four, I'd say," Aborigine replies.

"We'll have to wake Crude and Shakespeare up. They won't want to miss this."

"What about Doc, Captain?" asks Patch.

"Sure, I guess we should wake him up, too. Though you tell me how he's going to help," replies Captain Tanner.

"Well, help help, I don't know. When's that lazy bastard ever helped with anything?" says Drill.

"I don't know what you're complaining about. He takes our blood pressure once a month," counters Patch.

"He's not even a doctor. Before they pinched him for reselling drugs on street corners, he worked as a vet's assistant," says Tripod.

"He tells good jokes," offers Patch.

"That's true," Tripod concedes.

"'What did the alien say to the garden? Take me to your weeder,'" says Patch.

"And when he snores in D major, it brightens up the journey," adds Drill.

"That too," says Tripod.

"Could you focus on the job at hand?"

"Yes, Captain. We're on the case," replies Patch.

3

Space Monitoring Centre
Houston
Local Time: 12.05

James Benson – doctor of philosophy in physics when he is on the university campus, aeronautical engineer during office hours, colonel if there are military personnel on site, poker player on Friday nights and baritone in the church choir on Sunday mornings – is peacefully reading the sports' pages in his office when David Hooper knocks and pokes his head around the door.

"Sir, I have an unidentifiable echo on my screen."

Colonel Benson is trying to assimilate the fact that the Red Sox lost, contrary to all expectations, costing him the 225 bucks he had expected to turn into 360. Those damn substitute defenders should be on the unemployment line.

"Reset the equipment, Hooper. Don't make me regret taking you off the bench."

"I've tried everything, sir. The equipment is working perfectly. It's an echo captured by the monitoring radars M21, M22 and M23."

"In Mars' outer orbit?"

"Yes, sir. Asteroid Belt Monitoring Service."

"What has it captured?"

"I don't know, sir. Whatever it is, it's not registered."

"It's not what?"

"It's not in our database, sir."

"It'll be a small asteroid. Maybe they'll name it after you. Miniasteroid Hooper. Calculate its trajectory and come back when you have it."

"I've already calculated it, sir. It doesn't have an asteroidal orbit.

"It doesn't? So what orbit does it have?"

"It entered the system at a hyperbolic tangent, sir. It reached the ecliptic with an entrance angle of seventy-one degrees, logging six million kilometres beyond Mars' orbit. In north-five gamma quadrant to be exact, sir."

"So it crossed the solar system and has moved towards the Southern Cross."

"No, sir. It slowed down, aligned itself with the ecliptic and has adopted an approach trajectory towards the inner planets."

"Take a cold shower and review the data."

"I don't need to review anything, sir."

James Benson stands up and pushes his chair away with such force that he nearly leaves its imprint on the wall. He is still a strong man, though almost old enough to ask for early retirement. While studying engineering at A & M University in Texas he played on the second line of defence in a few American football college league games, where they called him "the Butcher". Even now, approaching sixty, his arms are thicker than Hooper's legs. David Hooper is a mathematician with a doctorate fresh out of the oven and the corpulence of a long-distance runner.

"Let's go to your desk, smarty pants. It's been years since I cracked anyone's ribs and I've been missing it. Although in your case I'll have to restrain myself so as not to crush you completely."

Hooper's desk is more barren than a desert, with only a monitor, a keyboard and a touch screen clouding the horizon.

"Where's your calculator?"

"I don't use a calculator, sir."

"You want me to believe that you calculated a hyperbolic tangent without a calculator?"

David Hooper taps his temple.

"The best calculator in the world is up here, sir!"

"Good. That's better. With a man's voice. There's still time for you to grow on me, Hooper."

"Thank you, sir!"

Colonel Benson smiles. Deep down he is just a big old teddy bear, incapable of hurting anyone unless they are wearing a red Cougars shirt from Houston's varsity football team. But he gets so bored shut up inside an office that he needs to create a little drama.

I should've been a drill sergeant; at least I'd be out in the fresh air.

"Since when do you know how to talk like a sergeant, Hooper?"

"I didn't know I did, sir!"

Everyone else in the room looks up and laughs.

"What's the matter? Don't you have work to do?"

Everyone casts their gaze back to their monitors. James Benson sits in Hooper's chair and observes the screen.

"Get me a calculator."

The person at the adjacent table is already bringing him one.

Benson spends around twenty minutes making calculations. It has been even longer since he calculated Hohmann transfer orbits than when he last cracked some ribs. Moreover, this is not even a Hohmann orbit. When he has finished, he feels a cramp in the pit of his stomach, just like before beginning a match against a group of professionals who are paid a premium for each broken bone.

"Good God almighty, Hooper! Do you know what you've discovered, boy?"

"Yes, sir. I know. We have visitors!"

In his impeccable uniform, Colonel Benson rises and looks David Hooper up and down. He is wearing an old jacket over a Hawaiian shirt and ugly sandals the colour of a sick dog's mess.

"I reckon, Mr Hooper, that the big cats will want to meet you in person. The President himself might want to meet you in person. Are you going to introduce yourself dressed as a tropical waiter or try to fatten up a bit and I'll lend you a uniform?"

"The only military man is you, sir. The rest of us are civilians. Although we go with the flow, calling you sir and all that."

"Don't remind me."

I should be at Fort Benning boot camp, teaching the kids air transport 101.

James Benson returns to his office, goes to his desk, presses a button and enters his code. He has not closed the door, so everyone hears the strong, manly voice which makes the little old ladies cry on Sundays.

"Put me through to the Defence Secretary."

Without asking permission, Hooper enters the colonel's office.

"Sir, we've just proven that our civilization is complete garbage. We've discovered an extraterrestrial spacecraft which has aligned itself with our field and is coming towards us. A vessel which may have been travelling through space for centuries from God knows what star. A vessel whose scientific and archaeological value is impossible to calculate. And who do you call first? The Defence Secretary!"

"Stop living in the land of the fairies, Hooper. Who do you think pays our salaries?"

4

Aboard the Cargo Spacecraft Antipodes
Time on the spacecraft: 18.00

"My dad was so wrong! 'You'll die of boredom.' Yeah, sure, boredom. I wish I was bored! Take that boredom and head first into a cosmic incident. Girls and boys, ladies and gentleman, roll up, roll up. Behold the Great Astral Event. A guided tour of the extraterrestrial spaceship. Morning and matinée shows. Dare to look the Great Martian in the face. Don't forget your slingshot, just in case."

"Shut up, won't you, Drill? You're giving me a headache. There's no way I can activate the right grid like this."

Aborigine is handling a contraption that looks like a showcase of luminous coins randomly scattered in the gap formed by two parallel transparent sheets joined at the corners. It bears a passing resemblance to the age-old game of connect four. The sheets are in front of his face, like a floating screen, and his fingers slide the coins around. They change colour and location, while glowing digits appear and disappear next to them in synchronisation with the appearance and disappearance of images and graphs on the two secondary screens.

On the main screen there is a constant central image of an object about the size of a shoebox with smooth walls the colour of lead shell casings and no identification lights.

"It looks nothing like a shoebox. It still looks like a coffin to me."

"Here we go again. You're such a pain, Crude."

Mike Gould has skin so black that he says it is the colour of petroleum, so everyone calls him Crude. When he is concentrating on a particularly tricky task, he can be heard speaking softly to himself, "Come on, Crude, you can do this."

"If it looks like a coffin to me, what do you want me to say? That's what it looks like: a coffin."

"'Sweet flower, with flowers thy bridal bed I strew,—
O woe, thy canopy is dust and stones!—
Which with sweet water nightly I will dew,
Or wanting that, with tears distill'd by moans.
The obsequies that I for thee will keep
Nightly shall be to strew thy grave and weep.'"

"Save us the poetry, Shakespeare, you're a pain too."

Andres Yarza, a diminutive man who would resemble a haughty little mouse if his budget stretched far enough to be well dressed, was a former professor of Universal Literature. When he taught, he loved to stress the 'Universal'.

"I don't just teach English literature, or Spanish, or French, or Italian, or Russian. No, no, I teach all of them. And do you know why I can teach all of them? Because I love them all equally. Because all literature delights me, regardless of from whence it originates. I wouldn't want to leave anyone out. I would faint if someone forced me to choose between Cervantes or Tolstoy. I would have a heart attack if I could no longer read either Garcia Marquez or James Joyce. Because I would be dumbstruck if I had to express a preference between *The Hive* and *The Trial*. Because all the books I've read form part of my soul. That is why I can teach all literature."

They say his students adored him and no doubt it is true, he is a good man. But he committed the inexcusable blunder of falling head over heels in love with a fifteen-year-old pupil. After spending a term making a fool of himself by following her up and down the corridors, composing sonnets and presenting her with bunches of flowers, he received his marching orders. After his dismissal came a year of which he remembered nothing more than the sensation of floating and a stinging nose. Then came the third stage: seven months of detoxing and advice from his psychologist: "You need some manual labour to keep your mind busy." He recalled having studied mechanics for a spell, but it is not entirely clear to him how he ended up in the space debris service.

"I am not a pain. I am a scholar fallen on hard times."

"If you all stopped yapping so much, maybe I'd get it right."

It seems as though Johnny Wash needs a couple more fingers to handle the tracking device properly.

"If you're clumsy, you're clumsy. Don't try and put the blame on us, goldilocks."

"When I've got a second, I'm going to punch your lights out, Crude. If I just had a decent tracker, not this old relic."

"Two years ago it was the last word in trackers. You

said so yourself, Aborigine."

"I know, Captain, I know. But in the past couple of years they've perfected the dual azimuth inertial platforms and the parasitic wave discriminators. You can't even play Congo Bongo with this prehistoric piece of crap."

Just as he says this, the discs stop moving and turn yellow. Blue and black lines spread across the touch screen Aborigine was fiddling with.

"Yeah! I'm a beast!"

"Good. That's my boy."

"Target fixed, Captain."

The image of the visitor is more defined on the screens and they can see it from different angles, as if they had several drones flying around it. It is no longer just a simple box with smooth walls; they begin to discern structural elements. Now they can see filigrees on the side which seem to be decorative and a narrower structure on top of the main body looms into view. It appears to have lots of windows, like portholes on a boat.

"Estimated time for dropping anchor?" asks the captain.

"I don't know. I reckon we could start to board her in a couple of hours."

"Don't say it as if we were pirates."

"Sure, what was I thinking? We're garbage collectors. A whole other level."

"Wait!"

"What's gotten in to you, Crude? Why are you yelling?" asks the captain.

"I've got it! I know what it reminds me of and it's not a coffin."

"Finally. Just as well."

"It reminds me of a sarcophagus. Can't you see the resemblance? It's like an Egyptian sarcophagus. The ones with the rotting mummies inside."

"Stop with the mummies and the coffins," says Drill. "I'm the one who has to board it and take a look around later. And that jalopy is probably darker than Darth Vader's boxers."

"Who on earth is Darth Vader?" asks Yarza.

"It doesn't matter, Professor. The point is that there's probably less light inside that thing than in the catacombs."

"'A grave? O no, a lantern, slaught'red youth;
For here lies Juliet, and her beauty makes
This vault a feasting presence full of light.
Death, lie thou there, by a dead man interr'd.'"

"Don't bust a nut, scholar fallen on hard times."

"Hey, where's the doc?" asks the captain.

"Still sleeping," replies Crude.

"What a guy. He sleeps more than a cat," says Tripod.

"He is Sleeping Ugliness. You'll have to give him a kiss," Patch jests.

"Yeah, right. Not even with a mask on," says Crude.

5

Space Monitoring Centre
Houston
Local Time: 18.00

"Come on, Hooper. Turn that gizmo off, would you?"

"Sorry, sir."

The five other civilian technicians on the first shift are standing at attention. Well, more or less at attention. Only Hooper is still at his desk. Right up until the last possible minute, he is checking his voicemail messages and activating some extravagant polarised grids that nobody has ever used.

Colonel Benson is also standing at attention, only more so than the others and facing them. The emaciated Hooper does not stand out for his slender frame: he is neither the skinniest nor the gawkiest. Benson's main team consists of three mathematicians, two engineers and an astrophysicist who do not even know how to spell the word fitness. They are a new breed of men: they have grown up in their swivel chairs, eyes fixed to the screen, finding keyboard shortcuts with both hands. They detect errors in a matrix calculation program two minutes after unwrapping it, they know how to handle the strangest gadgets without even glancing at the instruction manual and they can figure out how to activate options which do not appear on the menu, but they would be incapable of running three laps around an athletics track. Colonel Benson observes them. *They wouldn't last ten seconds on the Cowboys' field*. He keeps his thoughts to himself, partly because the Dallas

Cowboys ground as he knew it no longer exists. The new virtual betting system has turned it all into Philippine whorehouse.

Even the religion of the oval ball, which is the most sacred thing in this crazy universe. Oh Lord, it's enough to make you sick. Those scoundrels have no respect, not even for their own mother. They don't even respect the most sacred thing in this godforsaken world: the noble temple of the hundred-yard line. European rugby is the only sport that's hanging on in there come hell or high water, still being played on the classic and beloved grass pitches. Pity I never did understand those maddening English rules.

He looks at Hooper. It seems he has managed to fix himself up a bit, finding a dark suit and black shoes from somewhere and combining them with a horrendous multi-coloured tie that looks like a display of raw pizzas.

"Hooper, if you'd have managed to find a decent tie to go with the suit, I'd kiss you on the lips."

"In that case, I'm glad I didn't, sir."

Everyone smiles, even Benson.

"Less grinning, boys, less grinning. Today could be a big day for us or the day we screw it all up. The Defence Secretary can't be here in person, as he's in a meeting with the President, but he's sending us his right-hand man, his main advisor, Mr Benjamin Fischer. Unfortunately, Mr Benjamin Fischer is a lawyer. In other words, if he has to multiply two by three, he probably asks for help. We are going to explain everything to him very clearly. No technical jargon. No numbers. No long words. No mention of coordinates, quadrants, trajectories, vectors, waves or anything that sounds like physics or engineering or any other mode of thinking related to a higher intelligence. Think of him as a caveman or somebody with learning difficulties. Got it?"

"Yes, sir," a voice replies.

Taking advantage of the fact that he measures a little over one hundred and fifty centimetres, Benjamin Fischer has slipped in through a side door without anyone noticing. He is a slight, elderly gentleman with completely white hair and matching beard. To resemble Santa Claus, he would only have to dress up in a red suit and gain about four hundred pounds.

"Mr Fischer," Benson says, approaching the new arrival and offering his hand. "I trust you will forgive my outburst."

Benjamin Fischer stretches his arm up and places his little doll hand into Benson's ham-like fist.

"Six," he says.

"I beg your pardon?"

"Six. Two times three is six. If I am not mistaken."

"I'm glad you see the funny side. I apologise again."

"No need. To tell the truth, I do need an explanation without too many vectors. Start by introducing me to your team."

"Kramer, Stephenson, McBride, Hooper, Sorensen and Zimmerman."

Benjamin Fischer shakes another six hands.

"And now," he says, "show me the picture."

"The picture?"

"Yes, of course. The picture. The picture that's brought me here in such a rush from Washington as if the Martians were attacking."

"Yes. Of course. This way, please. Look. This is the monitor Doctor Hooper was working at. He was the first one to... Hooper! What the devil have you been doing?"

"Sorry. I'll fix it right now."

Hooper simultaneously presses a combination of three letters and most of the grids, lines, points, markers and alerts disappear. Only the orbital indication, the angular counters and a bright dot in the middle of the screen remain.

"Is that the visitor? That dot?"

"Yes, sir," says Hooper.

"Can't you make it bigger, with a little more detail? Is it just a dot?"

"I'm afraid it's almost in the asteroid belt, sir. Too far for anything other than radar identification and an approximate trajectory calculation. The image doesn't even correspond to a telescopic camera: it's a virtual image. The computer generates it based on the information it receives from the radar systems. Basically, the ones on Mars," Hooper explains.

"Virtual? Do you mean I'm seeing something that doesn't exist?"

"It exists, but the image isn't visual, it's virtual. It doesn't come from a camera," interjects Benson.

"So how do we know that that yellow dot is an extraterrestrial vessel? What if it's a natural object?"

"Well, in the first place, because the trajectory isn't asteroidal," says Hooper.

"Is there any chance it could be a natural object? Yes or no?"

"I'm pretty sure it isn't," says Benson.

"Pretty sure?" enquires Fischer.

"Um, we can't be one hundred per cent certain, but..."

"No. There's no chance," interrupts Hooper.

Colonel Benson shoots him a glare that could penetrate a lead wall, but Benjamin Fischer does not seem to mind. He turns towards Hooper.

"You're David Hooper, aren't you?"

"Yes, sir."

"Mathematician?"

"Yes, sir."

"Nice tie."

"Thanks. I can get you one, if you like. The Chinese store opposite is giving them away."

"Perhaps some other time. Right now, I'd prefer it if you could explain why it can't be a natural object. And remember your boss's orders: explain it to me as if I had half a brain."

"It can't be a natural object because the scrap merchants are already moving towards it."

"I think I'd prefer vectors. Did he say scrap merchants?"

Mr Fischer turns to Benson.

"What are you talking about, Hooper?" asks Benson.

"Allow me to show you."

Hooper sits down at his desk. His fingers move so fast over the keyboard that nobody can make out the parameters he is activating. Axes, figures, formulas and groups of dots appear and disappear on the screen.

"You'll see. We basically spend our time watching what a bunch of flying rocks are doing."

"It's a pleasure to hear how well this kid understands things," comments Fischer. "He really seems to want to explain things as if I were stupid."

Colonel Benson turns as red as he did that afternoon forty-four years ago. They had gone to train at some new facilities for the first time and the labyrinth of corridors must have confused him because he pushed a door open thinking his team was on the other side of it only to find himself in the middle of the girls changing rooms. He was fifteen at the time. The twenty or so basketball players were in the showers. He heard a door slam and then a voice yelled, "Girls, we have an admirer." Between them, they tore his clothes off, pinched him all over and shoved him naked into the corridor. A charitable soul lent him a towel. By the time he had finally managed to convince the coaches that he had gone in by mistake, it was almost night-time. It took quite a bit longer still for his clothes to appear. They had scrawled "cutie-pie" on his underwear in lipstick, along with a list of ten or twelve phone numbers. The worst came later when his mother found his briefs.

David Hooper, however, is unperturbed. He continues the explanation with the same nonchalance as if he were talking to a group of secondary school pupils; one of those groups that seem to be walking sponsors for the before half of an acne cream advert and who are occasionally found wandering around the space monitoring centre accompanied by science teachers who do not know the difference between a meteorite and a frozen fish finger. "You must catch a lot of channels with that antenna," a little old semi-retired lady had once said, pointing at the primary radar emitter. One sometimes hears an unreflective voice discrediting the work done by these teachers. As if it were no small thing to spend an entire school year with dozens of raving lunatics without committing murder.

"Thirty or forty of these lumps truly deserve to be called rocks, two hundred or so are nothing more than small stones and several thousand belong to the category entitled 'gravel scattered by the Lord in a completely random way'. Do you follow me?"

"I think so. Relax, Colonel. I assure you I like this kid. He reminds me of my grandson. Please continue to enlighten me, Doctor Hooper."

"There are lots of other teams tracking space, but we don't interfere with them because we're looking for different objects and we use different bandwidths. We are concentrating so hard on the lumps of rock that we don't stop to think about the vast number of vessels travelling around up there: they're filtered before the sweep appears on the screen. You see? If we change the filters, the rocks disappear—the yellow dots—and we see the blue ones, the spacecraft."

"That doesn't matter, Hooper," interjects Benson.

"No spaceship can travel that far."

"I'm afraid you are mistaken, Colonel. I've taken the liberty of exchanging a few messages with Space Traffic Monitoring. They look at spacecraft; we look at rocks. The information exchange tends to be automatic. The trackers inform Traffic Monitoring about the location of the rocks and the established limits for safe routes, but they don't tell us if someone is going outside these limits at some point, nor do we care. We're like hydrographers: we indicate where the reefs are, then it's every sailor for himself."

"Get to the point, Hooper," says Benson.

"The cargo ship *Antipodes*, which hunts and captures the junk metal floating around in space, was roaming around the Mars orbit, precisely where it shouldn't be roaming. We've added quite a few extensions to the Mars orbit station lately; in fact, it's nearly a complete toroid now. Quite a few kilos of metal have probably been left in space, which is a massive risk, so they pay the merchants to..."

"Get to the point!"

"That thing entered the ecliptic right in front of their noses."

"And they have detected the... visitor?"

"Absolutely. They've turned off their radio beacon and transmissions. They'll say that they've lost the antenna alignment because of a fifteen-cent screw. The old trick that Clarke used in *2001: A Space Odyssey*. In any case, two plus two makes four. If they've cut the ties it's because they don't want to share their find with other merchants."

"Supposing this unknown object is an extraterrestrial vessel of inestimable value," says Fischer. "The *Antipodes* plans to tow it back to Earth, right?"

"No, sir, not exactly. I don't think they operate that way. I don't think they have the slightest inclination to tow the craft intact. Among other reasons, because if we've detected it from so far away, it must be bigger than the cargo ship. Right now they're probably arguing about how to start pulling it to pieces."

"Pull it to pieces? We have to send them a very clear message: 'Don't touch a thing.'"

"I don't see how, sir. Traffic Monitoring have confirmed that they are incommunicado."

"Who's in charge of the cargo ship?"

"One William Tanner. I've asked for his file, but so far they've given me nothing but excuses. All we have is his name and rank: William Henry Tanner, Navy Lieutenant."

Benjamin Fischer turns from Hooper to face Colonel Benson.

"Colonel, are you aware that at this very instant, here in this room, I have the honour of representing the President of the United States of America?"

"Of course, sir."

"Then get me Lieutenant William Tanner on the phone. And I am not accustomed to being kept waiting. Understood?"

"Loud and clear, sir."

6

Aboard the Cargo Spaceship Antipodes
Time on the spacecraft: 18.30

"Can someone tell me how we're going to pull that beast apart?"

"I'm thinking, Crude, I'm thinking," answers Aborigine.

"I think we should hook it up and tow it in one piece," says Patch.

"We don't know how much it weighs yet," adds Drill.

"I'm on the case," says Aborigine. "But I reckon it's at least a hundred thousand tonnes."

"That's crazy! We can't tow that monster, Patch," says Crude.

"Well, that's the best option in my opinion."

"Even if we could," says Drill, "what happens when we enter the earth's atmosphere? Do we just let it fall?"

"You see? We can't get back to Earth with that hulk attached to us," echoes Crude.

"We could take what we can now and mark the rest with a system of automatic tracking buoys. You know, the ones that emit a pulse with a preset frequency. We'd be the only ones who could detect it," suggests Tripod.

"The Chinese have dynamic echo trackers. We'd come back to find a red dragon with a sign saying

'Thanks, dumbasses'," says Drill.

"Plus, we're really far out. We can't just come and go in a jiffy like it's our local food store. We'd have to calculate the fuel costs carefully. We might get bread instead of cake," adds Captain Tanner.

"What, Captain? Bread instead of cake?" asks Tripod.

"Yeah, it's a Spanish saying I heard once. You think you're baking a cake but when you open the oven, it's just bread. The best laid plans, and all that."

"And what have the Spanish got to do with it?" wonders Patch.

"I had a Spanish partner once, years ago, when I used to help Mexicans jump the fence. The Spanish guy interpreted for me. He was a great guy, but he was really unlucky in business. I was glad when he disappeared."

"Why is no one listening to me?"

"Okay, Tripod, go ahead. We're listening."

"Thanks, Captain. We'll have to set it in a Lagrange point that holds it in Mars' orbit."

"They'll see it in a heartbeat," says Drill.

"Let me finish."

"They're going to see it."

"Shut up, Drill. Let him explain," the captain orders.

"We'll use the Lagrange point as a reference and set it in geostationary orbit over a radar blind spot. Then we can take it apart over ten, twelve or twenty trips. There's no other way."

"I'm telling you, they're going to see it. By the third trip we'll have fourteen hundred Chinese vessels on our tail. Let's take what we can now, let it float away and move on to the next find," insists Drill.

"And where do we start?" asks Patch.

"With the engines. They're always worth the most."

"Do we know where the engines are or what, idiot?"

"We'll look for them."

"Listen up. I've nearly got the exact dimensions. There. Got it. Whoa, the computer was way off with the preliminary estimate of three hundred metres. That's weird. It's never been so far off."

"Get to the point, Aborigine."

"Length: four hundred and eleven metres. Breadth: sixty-eight. Height: forty-one. Then there's some kind of covered bridge that protrudes three metres."

"That's a monster! We're talking about a million tonnes. Maybe much more," says Tripod.

"Where the hell did such a beast come from?" asks Crude.

"Even more importantly: what the hell is it?" adds Drill.

"Got it," says Aborigine. "Sixty-six thousand six hundred tonnes."

"That's nothing!" exclaims the captain.

"That can't be right. It's way too light," says Tripod.

"It must be completely hollow," Aborigine conjectures.

"Shit. Just what I needed to hear. Completely hollow. I keep telling you, it's a fucking coffin, man. It's a fucking death box. And it's got the proportions of a coffin, right?" Crude is near hysteria.

"You've watched too many horror movies," says Patch.

"You're getting on my last nerve. Stop fucking talking about dead people, will you?"

"Drill's right. Enough with the horror stories," Captain Tanner intervenes. "Didn't your parents ever tell you that talking doesn't fill your belly? Let's get back to business, guys. How are we going to take it apart?"

"I told you. We have to go for the engines and leave the rest," repeats Drill.

"Ready to anchor in thirty minutes," Aborigine says.

"Good. Let's see if we can do something useful and drop the chitchat."

"But, Captain, listen a second. How can it only weigh sixty thousand tonnes? It's too light. A hulk that size should weigh a whole lot more. Even if it is hollow. Are the walls made of paper or what?" asks Tripod.

"Wood. Boxes for stiffs are made of wood," insists Mike Gould.

"You're driving me nuts. And what's up with you?" Drill turns to Andres Yarza. "You look like you're in cloud cuckoo land."

The professor comes round from his reverie and clears his voice before speaking, "Gentlemen…"

"Add some more drama, why don't you?" says Drill.

"Gentlemen..."

"Let it out, Professor."

"There are decimals on the screen. It doesn't measure four hundred and eleven metres."

"Four hundred and eleven point four eight. Width: sixty-eight point five eight. Height: forty-one point one four. Then an eight. Would sir like more decimals? Tough. There aren't any."

"Convert it to feet please, Aborigine."

"Okay. In feet... Holy shit! One thousand three hundred and fifty. Two hundred and twenty-five. One hundred and thirty-five. No decimals!"

"Explain yourself, Shakespeare," says the captain.

"The English foot is a highly illustrious measurement of length. It is inherited directly from the sacred Babylonian cubit, which is also the father – the father, I tell you – of both the Egyptian and Hebrew cubits, the latter of which was used in Genesis."

"You're having us on, man," says Aborigine.

"I'm not 'having you on'. This thing is designed in Hebrew cubits. That's why the numbers in English feet are exact numbers, with no decimals. And, by the way, now I'm absolutely certain that it's hollow inside. It may even be made of wood."

"Come on, man, stop guessing," says Patch.

"One to six and one to ten."

"Talk sense, for fuck's sake," says Drill.

"The proportions of Noah's ark!"

"Just what I needed to hear," says Crude.

"You've gone too far this time, Shakespeare," says Tripod.

"I've got a first approximation from the ultrasound scanner," says Aborigine. "I'm sending it to the right-hand screen. Is it clear? I'm going to put it in high contrast now. There. Can you see it? It's practically hollow. The inside is divided into three decks; each one is forty-five feet high. The outside is a sealed monohull system, seemingly of one piece. With no joins. I can make out a single entry point on the port side. It's at the height of the second deck, so you might say the lower level is the basement or the hold."

"Isn't there another entry point on the bridge on the roof?" inquires the professor.

"Um, yeah. In front. But it's much smaller. If it didn't sound so ridiculous, I'd say it looks like a porthole for the helmsman."

"Chapter 6, verses 13 to 22: *'And God said unto Noah, The end of all flesh is come before me; for the earth is filled with violence through them; and, behold, I will destroy them with the earth. Make thee an ark of gopher wood; rooms shalt thou make in the ark, and shalt pitch it within and without with pitch. And this is the fashion which thou shalt make it of: The length of the ark shall be three hundred cubits, the breadth of it fifty cubits, and the height of it thirty cubits. A window shalt thou make to the ark, and in a cubit shalt thou finish it above; and the door of the ark shalt thou set in the side thereof; with lower, second, and third stories shalt thou make it.'*"

"You know it by heart?" says Drill in wonder.

"'And, behold, I, even I, do bring a flood of waters upon the earth, to destroy all flesh, wherein is the breath of life, from under heaven; and every thing that is in the earth shall die. But with thee will I establish my covenant; and thou shalt come into the ark, thou, and thy sons, and thy wife, and thy sons' wives with thee. And of every living thing of all flesh, two of every sort shalt thou bring into the ark, to keep them alive with thee; they shall be male and female. Of fowls after their kind, and of cattle after their kind, of every creeping thing of the earth after his kind, two of every sort shall come unto thee, to keep them alive. And take thou unto thee of all food that is eaten, and thou shalt gather it to thee; and it shall be for food for thee, and for them. Thus did Noah; according to all that God commanded him, so did he.' I know the whole of Genesis by heart, down to the last comma."

"The whole of Genesis. By heart. Fuck, man, you *are* scary, not like Crude with his sarcophagus shit. My dad warned me about guys like you: 'Avoid three types of men like the plague: those who frequent hookers, those who gamble and those who read the Bible.' Go figure. A travelling companion who knows it by heart."

"So the cubit in the mind of the person who wrote the Bible is an exact multiple of the English foot. That's freaky!"

"Well, that's the way it is, however strange it may seem to you, Aborigine. The biblical cubit is exactly half an English yard, which is three feet. Likewise, the Hebrew and Egyptian cubits are complementary to the metre. Their sum total is equal to our current metre. Which indirectly implies, without stressing it too much, that whoever decided the Babylonian patterns of length knew the exact measurement of a modern metre."

"Come off it, Shakespeare. Even my granny wouldn't believe that," says Tripod.

"Well, tell your granny that it's the absolute truth."

"Captain, are all these conversations recorded in the flight log?" asks Patch.

"What does that matter?"

"If they sell copies to psychiatry students, I want a cut."

"Hold on, wait just a second. Didn't you hear the most important part of what Shakespeare said? Complementary to the Egyptian cubit," asks Crude.

"That doesn't mean a thing."

"What do you mean it doesn't mean a thing, Drill? Open your eyes, man. This is some bad juju, guys, I'm telling you. Bad, bad juju. I keep telling you it looks like a sarcophagus. And now it turns out it's measured in cubits. It's a load of mummies, guys, it's a fucking load of gutted dead people."

"Keep it up and you'll be exploring it by yourself," says Drill.

"There's no way I'm going in that thing! Not alone, not with you, not with Cleopatra's damn mother! I wouldn't set foot in there even if I had a battalion of green berets with me!"

"Did someone say they don't want to get paid?"

"Don't start messing with my salary, Captain. And don't make me go in there, however badly you want me to. I'm telling you, I'm scared shitless."

"You're kidding, Crude. Are you seriously telling me you're scared? For God's sake, we're so big we're the ones who scare other people. Relax, my friend. Whatever that vessel is, wherever it came from, there's nobody aboard."

"Look at this before you say anything else, Captain."

"What am I looking at, Aborigine?"

"Look at the scanner for the hold. See? Wait, I'm going to increase the contrast. There. Can you see them? Hundreds of objects lined up."

"They could be support buttresses. The equivalent of welding between the wall and the floor."

"Sorry, Captain," Aborigine interrupts, "Look at it when I zoom in. They're not touching the wall. Each object measures... Wait while I change the scale... About seven feet long by almost three feet wide. The size of a coffin. And there's a lot of them."

"Those are no dwarves," says Yarza. "Those are XXL coffins."

"Bad juju, guys! Thousands of dead dudes lined up in rows! Thousands of mummies! Bad juju, guys, bad juju! Let's get out of here. Seriously, let's go while we can. We've got to get out of here!"

"Shut it, Crude! You're making me antsy, too. Absolute silence! Listen, I'm going to explain something in simple language even a child could understand. I'm broke. Got it? Ruined. Destitute. Not a cent to my name. The loan sharks have sucked me dry. I invested my last cent in this flight. If we go back empty, I won't even be able to buy you a beer. See where I'm going with this?"

HORUS

William Tanner takes a breath that swells his chest. He is an impressive man: when he raises his voice, he resembles a wild bear ready to kill with a single swipe of his paw. Everyone listens in silence.

"I don't give a fuck if they look like coffins. I wouldn't give a fuck if they were coffins. And I still wouldn't give a fuck if the rotting corpse of a bishop and his favourite altar boy were in each one of the damn things. We're going to board that vessel. We're going to unscrew everything that looks like it's worth more than a dollar. We're going to store it in the hold. We're going to fill it until there's no room for a flea's eyelash. We're going to go back home and we're going to sell everything to the highest bidder. And when we've sold everything and split the dough, we're going to go on a three-day bender. Got it..."

"Yes, sir!"

"... Or do you need me to draw you a map?"

"Captain, I'm thrilled. That was a speech worthy of Sir Winston Churchill."

"Stop naming weird people, Professor. And you, Aborigine, earn your pay: calculate a good approach vector."

"Already done. I don't waste time talking."

7

Space Monitoring Centre
Houston
Local Time: 18.45

"I need ideas, boys," says Benson, who has just called his friends to tell them there is no poker this Friday with the excuse that he has a bad toothache.

"Sorry," says McBride, a statistical analysis expert, "I have no clue how we're going to contact a spacecraft that's disconnected its antennae."

"There must be a way. I don't want to go see that midget and tell him 'Sorry, mister representative of the Defence Secretary, I'm not capable of accomplishing the mission you gave me.' I'd rather put my head in the garbage disposal."

"You'll have to think of something else. Your head wouldn't fit in the garbage disposal."

"Yours would, Hooper. Yours would fit just fine, so don't put any ideas in my head."

"It might not be such a good idea to get rid of me. I've just solved your problem. You can go to this guy and tell him loud and clear, 'Mission accomplished, sir.'"

"Seriously? Ask me for anything you want. I'd even marry you."

"Don't scare me, sir. It's really quite a simple problem. We can't call the *Antipodes*, but another spacecraft could."

"I don't understand."

"The auxiliary channel."

A light bulb goes on in Colonel Benson's head.

"You're a genius, Hooper. I need a list of candidates. It has to be a spacecraft that is close enough and has a human crew."

"I've already drawn up a list."

"You're even starting to look more handsome to me, Hooper. Come on, don't look so scared. Who's our best candidate?"

"This one. *Antarctica IV*. It's got five men on board. They've spent the past twenty days exploring the Mars satellites, Phobos and Deimos. *Antarctica IV* is about to start coming back to Earth. And, what a coincidence, their thrusters are going to fail."

"Who's in charge?"

"Colonel Alexei Ivanov."

"A Russian?"

"Yeah, why not? We've recruited a couple of thousand of them recently. They do a good job. And they're fucking masters at obeying orders without a fuss."

"Working with me is good for you, Hooper. You're learning more masculine vocabulary. How long will it take for us to be able to speak with Ivanov?"

"About thirty minutes. But I think there's another deadline that's more important."

"Explain yourself."

"How long is it going to take for the media to find out? That's a good one."

"One problem at a time. We'll think about the press later."

Forty minutes later, having congratulated Benson and his team, Benjamin Fischer sits in front of the communications monitor and says, "Colonel Ivanov, I am going to entrust you with a task of the utmost importance. Even though it may seem like a strange request, the task involves simulating a technical fault."

HORUS

8

Mary Sanchez's House
Houston
Local Time: 18.45

While Benson is explaining Hooper's idea to Fischer, Mary Sanchez is at home, pretending to blow out candles on an imaginary cake. It is her birthday. She is celebrating it with her two cats, the television and a photo of her parents, may they rest in peace.

"Happy birthday, Mary," she says to herself.

She cuts herself a slice of the fictitious cake and pretends to eat it while she watches the trash TV they are broadcasting on one of the national channels. She never watches the local channels; they are even worse.

I forgot to make a wish. So what? Only first-graders believe in that nonsense. You're a big girl now. Independent and a college graduate with a job everyone thinks is great. A big girl. Yeah, very big. Even bigger today. Thirty-two. That's so old! Even I can't believe it. It seems like yesterday I was in Ms Henderson's class, learning my times tables. Do you have the number of a good psychiatrist? There might still be hope. Perhaps I should go back to Mexico.

Mary has spent seven years working as a journalist and eighty months regretting it.

But what is it there that makes me feel so strange? I was so little when we came to Houston. Yeah, yeah, my parents had the best intentions. Why wouldn't they? They worked themselves to death. Never a truer word.

Drop it, Mary. Your father's not the only person ever to have fallen off a scaffold. And you're not the only person who lives alone in this great country. Don't start crying, sweetheart.

I have two cats that adore me. What have I got to complain about?

She ends up turning down the sound on the TV. She does it quite often, watching the images, as if hoping to find some meaning in them.

I'd forgotten how soft this chair is.

She closes her eyes for just an instant.

When she opens them, the brightness that had been streaming in through the window is blocked by an object. From a distance, it looks like a bus. A windowless, rectangular bus.

It's kind of like an Egyptian sarcophagus, except for the fact that it's gigantic.

It is descending from the sky. It is very dark. It looks like lead. It is a little scary.

Huh, that's strange. It's chosen to land in my garden.

There is a door on one side of it with a ramp that looks like it is made of wood.

That great big heavy thing has parked itself in my garden and reminds me of Noah's ark, so I've definitely gone crazy. I'll just go outside and walk up the ramp. I enter. I don't know what I'm doing here. There's a reddish light. There are objects lined up on the floor. They look like coffins. Thousands of coffins. I want to look inside one, but I'm scared. I move closer. I'm about to lift the lid. Oh my God, it's full of stars.

HORUS

The telephone wakes her up. She answers with the unmistakeable voice of someone who has just woken up.

"Hello?"

"Mary? Aren't you up yet?"

"I've been up for a long time, boss. Over twelve hours."

"I'm sure you have. I want to see you in my office first thing tomorrow morning. I've got a job for you."

Mary Sanchez started her career in journalism enthusiastically. She was even lucky enough to have started with a pretty good story about the treasure that had lain in a sunken Spanish boat forty miles off the coast of Norfolk for five centuries until it had been discovered by a Canadian diving team. Her boss has invited her to supper six or seven times but she has always declined. Lately, she has not been given anything more than third-rate hogwash designed to fill space before they published or broadcast and started thinking about the next day's headlines. Or the advertising text that appears for an instant in the corner of the screen and disappears before anyone has time to read it.

"What is it this time? Has someone killed their neighbour's dog?"

Dog. Dog. Did Noah have a dog? Noah's ark? What was I dreaming about?

"Well, I know I've only given you titbits for the past few months. But this time I've got some solid journalistic work for you."

"Really?"

"Really! I want you here at daybreak tomorrow."

"What's it about?"

"Are you into astronomy?"

9

Aboard the Cargo Spaceship Antipodes
Time on the spacecraft: 17.30

"Come on, guys, we want it today. Patch is going to fall asleep waiting for you to tighten four clamps," says Captain Tanner.

"Yeah, yeah, almost done. This compressor weighs a tonne."

"You waste your strength talking, Drill."

"Sure, it's my fault for not being Superman. Patch might be the pilot but, if you ask me, he could be helping me stick these auxiliary tanks in place."

"You shouldn't have taken them out in the first place," says Patch, still drowsy in the pilot's seat.

"What about you, Mike?" asks the captain.

"Pretty black."

"What's new? You still scared?"

"To death. But I'm also proud."

"That's what I like to hear. Aborigine!"

"Captain?"

"I can't see the tube."

"I'm on it."

"Come on, guys, let's go."

"Almost done, almost done. Always such a fucking rush. What about the tube?"

"Aborigine's looking for the switch."

"Funny as always, Drill."

"Tube connected," says Aborigine.

You might say this tube does not exist. Or that it is immaterial. Or that it is a field. Or that it is made of light. Green light in this case.

The closest comparison to leaving your own vessel to approach another one in space, millions of miles from any place to rest your feet, is that of diving overboard a boat in search of sunken wreckage at the deepest depths of the cold, dark ocean. You have to use highly complex equipment and respect extremely strict rules. Unforgiving rules. One mistake and you are dead. This is even truer in space. Two seconds after making a mistake, you are a block of ice and harder than marble. That is, supposing you are still in one piece. Supposing that your own blood pressure has not made you explode like a balloon full of blood and guts. So the tube is an aid, like the ropes sometimes used by divers so they do not get lost.

The mother ship, in this case the *Antipodes*, is a thousand feet from the target vessel following velocity equalisation. The advance party is in an oval module measuring no more than five metres across at its widest shaft. The crew comprises the pilot, Patch, and the two members nominated to board, Drill and Crude on this shift. The tube is a cylinder of light that connects the two vessels while the module glides along inside it. It serves as a guide for the pilot and is of greater psychological than technical use.

The curved, yellowish module brakes fifteen metres from the foreign vessel. It looks like a chickpea on a pool table.

"Launching probe," Patch announces.

The probe, invisible to the human eye, is a multi-frequency beam that partly bounces back to the transmitter, which has a detector. The part of the probe absorbed by the object it hits will tell the crew more about its nature.

"Wait for it," says Patch, eyes glued to the screens. "It's magnesium, almost completely pure. Not even two per cent impurities. The main materials are titanium and chrome. With traces of platinum."

"What kind of alloy is that?"

"No idea, Captain. The database has nothing like it. The magnesium coating is really fine, like paint. Underneath there's a structure made of... I don't know... some type of ceramic material."

"Permission for the explorers to abandon the module," says the pilot.

"Permission granted," says Captain Tanner, giving a sideways glance at Doc, who attempts to look like a professional medic as he nods sagely.

"Let's get this party started, guys," says Patch. "You have thirty minutes of oxygen. Ten minutes extra in the auxiliary. So you explore for twenty minutes and get back here. No messing around, no unnecessary risks. I don't want any heroes, I want men who think straight and do a good job. Understood?"

"Yes, mama. All work and no play," says Crude.

"Keep making jokes and you'll see how you end up, knucklehead."

Crude and Drill speed off towards the vast cosmic visitor. It is a turn of phrase: there is no atmosphere in the green tube.

"Don't worry, Patch. I know how to watch my back. You should have done the same, then you wouldn't be covered in patches."

"That's a good one. I won't laugh in case one of my stitches bursts."

"Are you ever going to tell us what really happened?" asks Drill.

"I've told the tale a hundred times: a white shark was chewing on me for a couple of minutes and then spat me out."

"Come on," says Gould.

"It's the truth."

"I don't believe a word of it. You've never been near water, not even when your mother christened you, you dirt bag. And sharks don't chew."

"Maybe it spat him out 'cause he's so filthy. My dad always said that..."

"That's enough! Concentrate on your mission."

"Aye aye, Captain. Establishing contact. Visual inspection of the target," says Gould.

"Can you see any rivets, joins, straps...?"

"Nothing. It looks like one seamless piece. The side is a sheet as smooth as a mirror, but there's no reflection; it's dark grey matt, no gloss at all. I've never seen anything like it. The closest comparison would be the lead colour they use for blank bullets."

"Well it's not lead," says Aborigine.

"I know, smartass. I was listening," Gould retorts.

"Is there even the slightest chance it's one of ours?"

"It's definitely not one of ours, Captain. God knows who made this thing. We're going to propel ourselves towards the door."

"Maximum precaution. Aborigine, you know the drill."

"Yes, Captain. Projectors at sixty per cent."

"You got enough light?"

"Plenty, Captain," replies Gould.

The module remains inside the green tube, but the two men move beyond it. Protected by their spacesuits and followed by the white spotlight controlled by Aborigine, they seem to hover over the immense grey wall. They look like two small silver mosquitos on the back of an elephant.

"We've reached the door. Wait for it, Captain," says Drill.

"What is it now?"

"What looked like a door from a distance now looks like a rectangle painted with a black marker. There are no joins, no border. The door is still just as smooth as the wall. In fact, there is no door, it's just a rectangular symbol painted on the port side."

"It still looks like a door from here," says Captain Tanner.

"I think it is a door. The thing is that this is what you

call really airtight, not like our vessels," comments Gould.

"There must be an emergency exit somewhere," says Patch.

"Try the window on top," the captain suggests.

"It's not worth it," Aborigine intervenes. "It's just as uniform as the door. No joins whatsoever. I can see it on the zoom."

"We're going towards the stern," says Crude.

"I'm right behind you. Keep the light on us, Aborigine," says Drill.

"Sure thing."

"And the oxygen reserves?"

"Good, Captain. Eighty per cent."

The diminutive flying insects hover over the huge back of the pachyderm.

"We're at the stern," says Crude.

"Bingo!" says Drill. "There are three hatches, one on each level."

"Calm down, they're just three round protrusions."

"I'm going to call them hatches, if it's all the same to you."

"Aborigine. Patch."

"Yes, Captain."

"I don't like this angle. I'm missing the movie."

"You've got the virtual monitor," says Aborigine.

"Screw the virtual monitor. Move us a little closer to the stern. Good. There, close enough. I can see them from here."

"Centring the tube."

"Okay, okay, got it."

"Oxygen?"

"Over sixty per cent. Relax, we're not martyrs."

"You think it's bad I'm worried?"

"No, Papa Bear."

"What did you call me?"

"I don't know," says Drill.

"He's forgotten," says Crude. "Fucking Alzheimer's."

"What a pair of clowns. Concentrate on the hatches. What kind are they?"

"Who knows? It looks like a doughnut welded in an arch. We'll have to apply pressure at the outer edge and pop it open, then we're in," says Drill.

"Isn't it screwed in?"

"There's nothing screwed in here. We'll have to detonate it to blow off the outer ring. Then we'll take off the entire hatch and go in. That way, we'll know how thick the walls are too."

"Around sixty centimetres according to the primary scanner," says Aborigine, who is still in the control room on the *Antipodes*, glued to his collection of monitors.

"I don't like making an entrance like this, Drill. I don't want to break it. Aren't there any clamps? No anchorings? Flanges? Plugs? Handles? Axles? Tabs? Disc or spring fasteners? Even an old hydraulic system?"

"In this restaurant there are no hamburgers or fried chicken, Captain. Only weird concoctions with God-knows-what in them. Like one of those old restaurants in Paris. Jesus, do you remember that shit? Pâté, gizzards, la coquille Saint Jacques?"

"Okay, I get it. Use the explosives, but don't make too much noise."

"Not to worry, Captain, nobody'll hear a thing out here and nobody's sleeping inside."

"Oxygen?"

"Enough. We'll open her up, take a quick peek and come back to mama so she can rock us to sleep with her tropical rhythms."

There is a hum. On the communications panel, two red lights start blinking.

"What the fuck is that?"

"The emergency channel. Captain, someone's calling us on the emergency channel," explains Aborigine.

"Shit. Aren't we switched off?"

"There's no way of turning off the emergency channel, Captain."

"I know, I know. Press the button and see what the hell they want."

"Spacecraft *Antipodes*? Captain William Tanner?"

"Speaking. Who are you? What do you want?"

"I am Colonel Alexei Ivanov, commander of the explorer spaceship *Antarctica IV*, initiating a manoeuvre of..."

"What are you doing on my emergency channel? Is it an emergency or not? You sound very calm."

"Colonel Alexei Ivanov here. Keep this channel open, please."

"What do you mean keep...?"

"*Antipodes. Antipodes.*" There is a moment of silence. It is evident it is a long-distance call and there is a time delay. "I know you can hear me, Captain William Tanner. My name is Benjamin Fischer. I am calling on behalf of the President of the United States of America. I'm calling you from the Space Monitoring Centre in Houston."

"Shit," says Captain Tanner in a voice that could carry a hundred metres.

"I am the representative for the Defence Secretary and I am speaking on behalf of the President, so I suggest you drop your bar vocabulary for a while, Captain Tanner."

"Shit, shit, shit. Is that better vocabulary, mister skinny cat representative of the fat cat? You owe me one, Ivanov. When I get my hands on you, you're going to wish you were being interrogated by the Russian secret service."

"Sorry, comrade. Money talks."

"No need to apologise, Ivanov. You can close your channel now. And you, Tanner, listen up. We know you have detected the intruder. We know you're situated about three hundred yards from it, give or take."

"I've got two of my guys working outside the vessel

as we speak."

"I just need thirty seconds of your attention."

"Pray that nothing happens to them."

"Let's get straight to the point. Your flight permit is American, so the intruder is the property of the United States Government. Therefore..."

"If you think it's yours, why don't you come and get it, big mouth?"

"Stop acting like a child. Sooner or later, you're going to want to land. Which welcome would you prefer: a cheque and a fanfare or a military police van?"

"You might be a representative of the President, but you talk like a henchman in the Sicilian mafia. What number will be on that cheque, Mister Corleone? Seventeen bucks?"

"Please don't think of me as a henchman, Captain Tanner, nor a tightwad. I have your financial details for the past year. At least, the ones you've declared. They're not bad at all."

"Deduct my men's wages, the repair bills, the million litres of fuel... Need I go on?"

"That won't be necessary. Let's not beat around the bush. If you tow the intruder intact and place it in the orbit I tell you, you'll have a nice fat cheque waiting for you. Last year's salary multiplied by three."

"Twenty."

"Five."

"Fifteen."

"Seven and I swear I won't go a cent higher."

"Deal. We'll reengage on channel 110. We're going to see if we can realign the antennae. Over and out."

Captain Tanner cannot help but leap into the air.

"Woohoo! Yeeeaaah! We're rich, guys!"

The captain turns to look at the four crew members with him aboard the command deck of the spacecraft *Antipodes*.

"Aborigine, Doc, Tripod, Professor, you want to tell me what's going on?"

The four men are glued to the spot with a stunned expression on their faces, staring at the main monitor.

Next to the vast body of the elephant, there are no longer any insects. Only the module remains, floating weightless in the green tunnel. Inside the module, against all regulations, Patch is standing up without his seatbelt on and with his nose pressed against the window like a small child.

A shiver runs down Tanner's back as he asks, "What about Drill and Crude? Where are they?"

"That thing swallowed them," says Tripod.

"What do you mean it swallowed them?"

"Just that, Captain. It swallowed them. A kind of bubble came out and, poof, in they went. Just like that."

"Get Module Two ready. Quick. Go, go, go."

"You won't fit in the module, Captain."

"I don't give a damn if I fit or don't fit. I'll hunker down and just put the thermal suit on."

"Without the pressure suit, you're a dead man, Captain. You can't go," Tripod insists.

"The day I abandon one of my men will be the day hell freezes over. Open the fucking capsule, Aborigine!"

"Calm down, Captain, please. I'll go, I'll go. Aborigine, see if you can open a parallel tube."

"I'm already on it."

Tripod is already pulling up a thermal suit over his padded one.

"Hurry up, for God's sake, hurry up."

"Module One now has audio," says Aborigine. "I'll put him on speaker."

"Patch? What happened?"

"I don't know, Captain, I don't know. A bubble took them inside."

"A bubble?"

"I don't know; it looked like a soap bubble. One second it was there, the next it was gone. The bubble engulfed them and went inside the vessel."

"But where?"

"I don't know; it sort of passed through the wall."

"I've got it in slow motion," says Aborigine. "Screen two."

In the middle of space, from the middle of nowhere, a dot of light appears. It is around the size of a small pea; a second later, the dot is as big and white as a golf ball; another second later, like a balloon inflated at great speed, it is almost as big as the module. It looks like a great plastic ball. The bubble approaches the two astronauts. What happens next is so incredible, so difficult to assimilate, that everyone looking at the screen turns whiter than a sheet, even Aborigine.

"Play it again," says Tanner. "Freeze it every tenth of a second."

Drill and Crude are in the image, next to the semi-transparent, silverish spherical bubble. In the next image, a tenth of a second later, only the bubble remains, still and silent with an infinitely innocent air. A further tenth of a second and the image shows two clearly human silhouettes inside the bubble. It moves towards the wall of the vessel and, strange as it seems, passes through it with the two captives inside. At least, there is no sign of anything outside the colossal machine except for the tube of green light and Module One.

The whole scene lasts less than six seconds.

They are left speechless. The only thing to be heard is Captain Tanner's heart. Ba-bum, ba-bum, ba-bum.

"The bubble!" shouts Aborigine. "It's coming out!"

"Tripod, come and take a look at this."

It's the same scene but in reverse, thinks Tanner.

There are two astronauts inside the bubble. In the blink of an eye the bubble is empty and the two men are floating next to it, adrift. The bubble shrinks to the size of a golf ball. Now it is a tiny white pea with its own light, a mother-of-pearl firefly glowing in the vast emptiness of space.

Patch is already manoeuvring Module One towards

the explorers. He hears voices and realises they are saying something to him, but he cannot make it out. He is too focused on the rescue mission. The module has various systems to recover personnel in difficulties and there had to be a first time to put them into operation.

"Activating electrostatic system," says Patch to himself in a low voice.

As he approaches them, the suits of the two men stick to the module's outer surface and the craft immediately sets off back to the mother ship.

"Open the entry gate!" yells Patch.

"All ready!" shouts Tanner, "All ready."

"Outer hatch open," says Aborigine.

The module enters the berthing gate with the two astronauts attached and apparently unconscious.

"Equalising pressure," comments Aborigine.

"Come on, come on. Close the hydraulics now!"

"I can't do it any faster, Captain."

"I know, I know. Come on, close the gate!"

"It's closing, it's closing. I'm not a magician. Twelve seconds. Eleven, ten... Two, one. Pressure equalised. Opening entry gate."

It is hard to see who runs faster. The crew lay Drill and Crude out on two stretchers. Doc checks their vital signs, opens their spacesuits and touches their eyelids. Crude opens his eyes, closely followed by Drill. They do not seem to be injured, only disoriented and confused.

"Guys..." Tanner's voice is barely audible; his body is

in shock. "Say something. Talk to me Mike."

Crude and Drill have slightly blurry vision. Crude is the first to speak.

"There are people inside that thing."

"People?"

"Yeah, people. Or weird creatures. Or floating ghosts. I'm not sure. Isn't that right, Drill?"

"Yeah, he's right. And you can't imagine how ugly they are."

Day 2

Saturday, 4 May 2030

"On a cosmic scale, only fantasy has any chance of being right."
Pierre Teilhard de Chardin.

HORUS

1

Heathrow Airport
London
Local Time: 08.30

Ted Howard had no idea that Doctor Mathias Shepard was the spitting image of Albert Einstein. The crow's feet, the long white hair, the moustache, the wrinkles on his forehead, the tiny chin, the curved eyebrows, everything the same, even the extra large nose.

He looks like a clone for heaven's sake. My sister could have warned me. Then I wouldn't be staring at him with this idiotic expression. I can't even blink. He must think I've got a screw loose.

"I think your sister's idea was an excellent one. Yes, indeed, a most excellent idea."

"Excuse me?"

"To make you come here. Your sister."

"Ah, yes. An excellent idea. Of course."

"I understood you were a specialist in genetics, not in moulds."

"In moulds you say?"

"Yes, a marvellous idea. Your opinion is of great interest to me. A good number of archaeologists have been tricked by this idea of moulds. As you know, a microscopic fungus grows on the wooden sides of the sarcophagi and inhaling it is what caused the death of those who violated Tutankhamun's tomb. The materialists are very satisfied when they hear this type of explanation: they prefer the word 'fungus' to 'curse'; spores instead of ghosts. As if they knew what a fungus is or understood what a spore is. We romantics prefer to continue using the word curse. Although the curse must select an active agent, a vehicle if you will, such as a fungus, a spore or a mould, wouldn't you agree? In any case, your presence here gives the project a touch of the interdisciplinary. And we all know how much our Vice-Chancellor likes that word, so if we want him to keep paying the bills, the least we can do is make him happy once in a while, don't you think?"

"Yes, yes. Of course."

"Although the students are saying that the Germans have poured a lot of money into this excavation. Heaven knows where they got such a nonsensical notion. Getting back to the matter of moulds and curses, I would compare it to that old joke, the one about the man stranded on his roof during a flood. The water keeps on rising but the man has faith that God will save him. Do you know it?"

"Um, no, I don't think so."

"Along comes a man in a boat. 'Climb aboard', he says. 'No thank you, God will save me.' Then a speedboat and a yacht appear. 'Climb aboard.' 'No thank you, God will save me.' A little later an army helicopter shows up and they throw down a rope ladder. 'Take a hold of the ladder.' 'No thank you, God will rescue me.' When the flood has risen above the house and only the man's head is above water, a submarine emerges. 'Climb aboard,' they yell from the turret. 'No, God will come and save me.' Finally, the water engulfs him and he drowns. He ascends to heaven and he is furious. 'I had faith in You,' he says to God, 'I had faith that You would rescue me, but You never came. You didn't lift a finger to save me.' 'I didn't lift a finger?' replies God. 'I sent you everything, even a submarine!'"

"I see. God manifests Himself through three-dimensional objects."

"Forgive me, I didn't mean to give you a lesson in metaphysics. I'm afraid I talk too much. Tell me what you're working on. Your sister mentioned you've just finished a project and that you're coming with us to study Egyptian microorganisms for a bit of a break before you start another one."

"Yes, something like that. Well... Hmm. Actually, I haven't just completed a project. I hate lies. The truth is that another researcher finished it first. A Japanese man: Doctor Kasigi. Hiroshi Kasigi."

"I understand how you must feel. Believe me, I understand all too well. At a conference, a Frenchman presented the complete translation of a funereal stone that I had been engrossed in for eight months. He finished the translation in five weeks."

"I've invested four years of my life in this project, six depending on how you look at it. And the ball landed on the zero. The house wins."

"I'm truly sorry. Can you tell me the nature of the project?"

"Have you heard of Dolly the sheep?"

"Of course. Everyone's heard of Dolly. You cloned

her."

"Well, not me personally: I wasn't even born then."

"Yes of course, I mean to say it was your university that cloned Dolly."

"That is correct. The same university, even the same department."

"And what have you been working on for the past six years? Cloning sheep?"

"No, that would be absurd. Cloning a sheep with today's technology has less merit than frying an egg."

"I see. So where does the merit lie nowadays?"

"In cloning a mammoth."

"A mammoth? Did you say a mammoth? But they are extinct!"

"Therein lies the merit."

"Perhaps I've spent too long among mummies and scrolls. I don't fully understand."

"There are thousands of mammoths in Siberia."

"Live ones?"

"No, of course not. Frozen ones."

"Aha! I see we work at opposite ends of the thermometer: here I am in scorching Egypt and there you are in frozen Siberia."

"Yes, opposite ends. There are thousands of frozen mammoths. Some of them, or rather lots of them are complete specimens, completely intact. There are several possible reasons for this, but I won't go into all of them. The most likely explanation is that there was such a sharp and sudden drop in the temperature that thousands of creatures froze solid with no carrion to feast on them. Anyway, the thing is that we can get enough mammoth tissue samples to try and revive the species."

"Revive or resuscitate?"

"I don't think resuscitate is quite the right word."

"And you say this Japanese doctor has succeeded?"

"Yes. As we speak there's a Siberian woolly mammoth alive and kicking somewhere in Tokyo. And there will be more, I promise you."

"And you've spent the last six years working hard, hoping that this mammoth would be born in Glasgow University."

"That's right."

"I was in Glasgow once. It was like living in a freezer, and that was in the middle of November. Considering the mammoth's comfort, my sympathies lie with you, not the Japanese doctor. And they say the Scots and the English don't get along."

"You might even say we share a mutual admiration."

"Of course we do."

"Thanks for the vote of sympathy. If you don't mind me saying so, it's very comforting. For the past few hours, I've been completely embittered by Doctor Kasigi's success. Embittered and disconcerted."

"Disconcerted?"

"Yes, disconcerted. And extremely curious. Doctor Kasigi hasn't published which part of the tissue he used to extract the necessary genetic material for the cloning."

"Does it matter?"

"Absolutely. The degree of chromosomal deterioration isn't the same for all tissue types. Freezing isn't instantaneous, so when the animal died, some tissues were damaged more quickly than others. Nor was it the same kind of damage. The nuclear membranes were broken in some tissues, but not in others."

"Fascinating."

"That's what I think."

"What tissues did you have your hopes of success pinned on?"

"I tried several lines of work. The most promising one was the epithelial, which is hardly surprising as the best-preserved tissue is always the deepest subcutaneous layer, the one touching the adjacent muscular tissue. It is always the tissue that stays most intact. After that, the muscle tissue itself, especially the striated tissue. Then there's the heart tissue, followed by the renal fascia. The other organs deteriorate too quickly, particularly the brain. The brain is rendered completely useless."

Doctor Shepard is rooted to the spot, rigid as a post. He stares unblinkingly at Doctor Howard.

"Doctor Shepard? Are you all right?"

"Sorry, I didn't mean to alarm you. It's just... I suspect you are unaware of how incredible it is for me to hear you reel off that list of tissues."

"I don't see why it is so incredible."

"Let me remind you that I have dedicated nearly forty years of my life to researching Ancient Egypt. Half the world considers me an authority on deciphering hieroglyphics, identifying mummies, finding tombs and a dozen or so other related matters."

"And?"

"There is a subject upon which I am honoured to be viewed as the leading authority in the world."

"And what subject might that be?"

"The embalming and mummification process."

"I don't see the connection."

"The tissue best preserved in Egyptian mummification is the deep subcutaneous tissue, which touches the muscles. Secondly, the muscle itself. During the first phases of the process, the embalmers extracted all the entrails, except for the heart and the kidneys, which they left in situ, so you could say that the mummy consists of the skeleton, muscles, skin, kidneys and heart. The intestines, lungs, stomach and liver were stored separately in four canopic jars, protected by the four sons of the god Horus. As for the brain, it was extracted and discarded, as if redundant, along with the nerve endings, including the optic nerves and eyes. Hmm, I see you have also turned pale, my friend."

"Hardly surprising. It's almost as if they wanted to conserve perfect specimens for subsequent cloning. Taking out the eyes is a good idea. They are two hotspots for humidity that can accelerate the putrefaction of the entire skull. But what did they do? Did they leave the sockets empty? That's not such a bright idea either."

"No, no. They filled the cranium with resin and put in two stones that matched the eye sockets as closely as possible. They washed them first with water, lime and vinegar. Then they bandaged everything."

"Two disinfected stones. Inert matter."

"Perhaps it is best not to draw hasty conclusions."

"That's always sound advice. When did the Egyptians start mummifying the dead?"

"Tradition has it that the first embalming was performed by the goddess Isis on her brother and husband, the god Osiris. Her other brother, Set, had buried Osiris alive in a sarcophagus, which he then dragged to the Nile so he would drown. So, to answer your question, we are talking about the time of Osiris and Isis. And to give them a timeframe, we must start by accepting their physical, tangible existence. You might think that a good example of rivalry is that which exists between rugby teams, during the Six Nations for instance, but I can assure you that it is as nothing compared to the rivalry between the Egyptologists who consider Osiris and Isis as mere mythological, unreal figures and those who believe they were flesh and blood, just like you and I."

"And which team do you support, if I may ask?"

"You might not find my answer satisfactory. Perhaps you will view it unorthodox. You are a scientist after all."

"I'm a biologist, not a physicist. My respect for scientific orthodoxy is no greater than my respect for my lab rats. I'd use Newton's *Principia Mathematica* to wrap a sandwich if I thought it might result in a new strain of bacteria, for instance."

"I see what you mean. And I share your philosophy. Nonetheless, I have the utmost respect for the extreme rigour exemplified by the work of physicists. I suspect that without them and their methodological strictness, we wouldn't have progressed beyond the steam boiler."

"Are you warming me up for a contradictory reply?"

"Indeed I am. I believe, and I ask for your utmost discretion on the matter, that..."

"My lips are sealed."

"... That Osiris and Isis were made of flesh and blood and as tangible as you or I, but that they were not human as we are."

"Holy mackerel! How does that work exactly?"

"The traditional story tells us that they were gods descended from the sky. When they reached Earth, they found humans living here that had barely evolved passed the simian stage, humans who were living off insects, seeds and leaves, and who resorted to cannibalism without the slightest remorse. Osiris, the protector god, taught mankind to clothe themselves, to cultivate vines, rye and barley, to make wine, bread and beer, to put sheep to pasture, to build houses and settlements, to write, to sculpt, to weave..."

"You wouldn't be talking about a couple of extra-terrestrials, would you now?"

"Why so shocked? I thought we had established that you were a biologist, not a physicist. Physicists—and we can probably blame the one bore a passing resemblance to myself—insist that interstellar distances are insurmountable, but a biologist shouldn't find it surprising that life found a way to expand in the universe. A biologist knows perfectly well that life expands everywhere and at any time. Look, here comes your sister. We'll continue our little chat some other time."

"I just have one question. I'm not sure I heard you right. Did you say that Osiris and Isis were both siblings and spouses?"

"That is correct. All the dynasties of the Egyptian civilisation have one constant: they were convinced that the perfect wife for a pharaoh was his own sister. So much the better if she were his twin. Egyptian texts lead us to believe that sexual relations between brother and sister were a common event and people thought nothing of it."

"Does my sister know this?"

"Of course she does. But it isn't a subject she likes to discuss. She is so shy and easily embarrassed!"

"Ha! You do know her well."

"Shh. Here she comes. She'll hear us."

"My ears have been burning for a while. Were you enjoying explaining all my faults to my brother, Doctor Shepard?"

"Well I never, Doctor Howard. How could you even think I would do such a thing? I consider you more divine than human. I've been praying not to fall into the sin of idolatry every night since I met you."

"Och, I do love your compliments, Doctor Shepard. Come on, the plane is waiting. I've managed to persuade the commandant that my entire luggage can fit. Didn't take me that long to convince him either, did it?"

2

Aboard the Cargo Spaceship Antipodes
Time on the spacecraft: 00.30

"Have you calmed down now?"

"Yes, I've calmed down."

"Don't be mad, Drill," interjects Captain Tanner. "Don't be mad. Doc is just doing his job."

"Well, he's been doing his job for an hour and a half. I reckon that's enough touching, injecting and suctioning. I've had it with this stretcher and all the needles, cardiographs and the rest of this bullshit."

"That goes double for me," says Mike Gould, who has been lying to the right of Nestor Sanchez since they were brought back to the *Antipodes* stuck to the belly of the module. "I'm so drained, I'm turning white."

They have spent the last ninety minutes in the medical unit: the two abductees, Captain Tanner, Doc, Patch, Yarza and Tripod. The only crew member missing is Johnny Wash, who is glued to the main console, endeavouring to decode the signals of the two cameras the explorers wore in their space helmets. The cameras had been recording the whole time, but for some reason he cannot see what they captured inside the intruder craft, which is still next to them, impassively maintaining a steady velocity and trajectory. Aborigine is trying everything he can possibly think of. He spent the first half hour testing different combinations of codecs to view the videos. Then he used video cross linkers and frequency exchangers, trying every possible permutation of updates and sampling. He tried compressing and decompressing different bandwidths, changing the interleaving audio parameters, slowing the video down, speeding it up, converting the image to black and white, increasing the colour, removing the contrast, increasing the contrast, applying the Doppler compensation program for remote transmissions. By the end of the first hour he had attempted every reasonable solution. Now he is in the 'desperate bordering on insane options' phase, which includes breaking down the entire video frame by frame and passing it through the image editor to assemble it as a timed presentation.

In a moment of absolute silence, Aborigine suddenly yelled, "I've got it!"

"Jesus, are you trying to scare us to death?" Drill grumbles.

"Get over here! I've found a way to view Crude's recording."

"For the love of God, you made me jump with that shout," says Tanner.

"Move!"

"We're coming, we're coming," says Patch.

"I'll show it on the two lateral screens."

"Move over, man, can't you see I need more room?" says Tripod.

"Are we going to start this thing or not?" asks Patch.

"Yes, yes," Tanner replies. "Hit play."

All they can see is a grey wall covering almost the entire screen. To the left they can just make out the green glow from the tube and a tiny part of the starboard side of the module. The camera turns to the right and captures something floating at Crude's side, something spherical and whitish, the size of a man. Up close, it looks like a living membrane, streaked with infinite blood vessels. Like the negative of a photograph of a bat's wing. Then there is no image at all.

"In that instant, you didn't exist," says Aborigine. "Nor did the camera."

"Sure, why not," reasons Crude.

Now the world is viewed from inside the translucent bubble. The camera moves in closer to the grey wall and in the blink of an eye it is inside. The bubble vanishes. The lens is floating inside the huge dark vessel. It is so voluminous it is overwhelming. Nine hundred Hebrew cubits long by one hundred and fifty wide and ninety high.

"You were on the lower deck, in the hold," comments Aborigine.

"How can you tell?" asks Drill.

"Everything matches what the scanner showed."

The space is semi-dark, lit only by a very dim reddish glow similar to the light during a night shift on a nuclear submarine, but even more tenuous. Objects can just be discerned. Lines of rectangular objects. The sensation that the hold is full of coffins is extremely disturbing.

"They're too big to be coffins. And too tall," says Gould.

"You're right. They must be at least one metre tall. Let's see, let me just measure it. I'm trying the millimetre grid. Got it! One hundred per cent confirmed. What unit do you want?"

"International System," says Tanner.

"Two hundred and twenty-eight centimetres long, ninety-eight centimetres wide and a hundred and five centimetres tall. Even you would fit in one, Captain. Maybe a little tight around the arms."

"I'll lose the gut."

"This is all giving me a very bad feeling," says Gould.

"Me too."

"Explain yourself, Professor."

"I don't know what to think. The external measurements of this artefact are of Noah's ark multiplied by three. In other words, twenty-seven times the volume of Noah's ark. That in itself is disconcerting. But the measurements of these boxes are just as famous, just as recognisable. I don't need to consult a database."

"Spit it out, man! Stop beating around the bush," says Tanner.

"Inside the Great Pyramid of Khufu, there are several chambers. One of them is known as the King's Chamber and in it lies a sarcophagus covered in quartz. It has the exact measurements that Johnny just gave us. If everything else matches Khufu's sarcophagus, the boxes won't have a lid and their walls will be fifteen centimetres thick while the bottom will be eighteen centimetres thick. That leaves a space measuring one hundred and ninety-eight centimetres long by sixty-eight centimetres wide and a height of eighty-seven centimetres."

"I'm hovering over a box. Yep, everything matches. There's no lid and all the measurements match, inside and out."

"Can we see anything inside them?" asks the professor.

"Zoom in if you can," says the captain.

"I'm trying," Aborigine pauses.

"There's something there. There are forty miniature boxes. In each box there are forty other boxes lined up on the bottom. But these little ones do have a lid."

"How big are they? What scale are they?" Yarza asks.

"One to twelve. Ordered in a five by eight matrix," says Aborigine. "Next to each little box there are four cylinders. Magnifying image. Fucking hell. Do you see what I see? They have engravings on them... They look like the heads of animals."

"Those are the four canopic jars," explains Yarza.

"The what?" asks Crude.

"The Egyptians buried four canopic jars with each mummy. They contained their entrails. I'm getting very nervous. It's as if each sarcophagus in the hold were designed to store the remains of forty people."

"In miniature?" wonders Drill.

"I don't know. It certainly seems like it."

"How many sarcophagi are in the hold? Have you counted them?" asks the captain.

"What am I, a magician? How could I count them so

quickly?"

"It's easy. Look, by rows there are ten groups of two and by columns there are ten groups of six. Each group has six times two or twelve sarcophagi. In total, the matrix is twenty by sixty. One thousand two hundred sarcophagi," says Tripod.

"A multiple of twelve," says Yarza. "And the groups are in twelves too. No surprise there, seeing as it's an artefact inspired by the Bible."

"I thought it was inspired by the Egyptians," says Crude.

"The Bible is Egyptian from start to finish."

"Sure, and the tango is Russian and pizza is Chinese," says Drill.

"The Bible is entirely Egyptian. I'm serious. The key character is Moses. The Bible tells us..."

There is a creaking. It sounds like the hull of a submarine when it dives to depths below its pressure limit. The creaking continues. It is as though someone has put the *Antipodes* in a pneumatic press. The monitors switch off and the lights blink.

"What's happening?" asks Patch.

They start to float, weightless.

"The centrifuge has stopped," says Aborigine.

The emergency lights come on, bathing everything in an orange glow.

"Everyone to their seats. Seatbelts on," orders Captain Tanner.

"Great, put more things in my way," Aborigine complains.

"You're just clumsy, that's why you're bumping into everything," says Crude.

"I'm going to bump your head with my fist."

"Aborigine, damage report," says the captain.

"No damage so far."

The lights come and go while the monitors emit snow and lines.

"Our friend has activated a magnetic field that runs circles around ours, right?" says Drill. "Am I right?"

"I don't know. The detectors have gone crazy."

"External view, Aborigine. We need an external view," says Tanner.

"Nothing's working. Wait, yep, we've got current again."

The lights stabilise. The centrifuge starts revolving again. The spacecraft has a floor on which to stand once more. Aborigine connects the cameras with an external view.

"External cameras on screens three and four."

At the prow only the sun can be seen as a yellow dot in the distance. The excessively imaginative say they can also make out the earth as a waxing quarter to the left. On the starboard side there appears to be a grey curtain.

"It's another bubble," says Crude.

"Yeah, it's another bubble like the one that

swallowed us up," confirms Drill.

This bubble is much larger, big enough to fit both vessels inside it. The prow cameras no longer show the sun; the only view is a grey curtain. All the systems reboot. The video recording starts up where it left off and Johnny Wash is once again surrounded by working monitors filled with graphs and tracers that sweep the screen.

"Captain, take a look at this."

"There's no way I'm taking my seatbelt off. Explain it to me."

"Spacecraft velocity: zero. All the speedometers show zero, like we've landed somewhere. But the absolute position indicator says we're moving at... Can you hear me?"

"Loud and clear."

"Five hundred kilometres per second and counting."

"Then why aren't we being flattened against the backrest?" asks Tripod.

"How should I know? I never even passed eighth grade physics. Direction?" asks Captain Tanner.

"Headed for interception with Earth's orbit. We could land in a couple of weeks."

"Jesus! It took us three months to get here."

"I'm calculating the acceleration and trajectory modification. Holy shit! We'll be there in less than a week!"

"Shakespeare, what are you doing with the calculator? Give it to me so I can hit you with it. You don't know how to calculate trajectories," says Tanner.

Professor tears his eyes from the screen.

"I'm just doing a multiplication. I must have done it twenty times or more."

"What multiplication?" asks Drill.

"Twenty times sixty times forty."

"You don't need a calculator for that. Forty-eight thousand," says Drill.

"Forty-eight thousand on each deck. Times three."

"One hundred and forty-four thousand."

"Yes, that's what it says on the screen. One hundred and forty-four thousand. The number that will be saved in the Apocalypse."

"You been drinking the alcohol from the first aid kit on the quiet?" asks Crude.

"It's not my fault it all adds up. Revelation says that one hundred and forty-four thousand people will be saved, twelve thousand from each of the twelve tribes. And this behemoth is hurtling towards Earth with one hundred and forty-four thousand containers in its belly, all lined up in boxes of forty and groups of twelve. Any second now we'll be hearing the trumpets of the Apocalypse, guys. And that thing travelling next to us is some kind of lifeboat."

"No more, please. That can't be right. There must be another, more rational explanation. Those boxes might be part of a circuit we don't understand."

"Hey, Drill, a minor detail," says Patch.

"What?"

"You said there were some ugly critters in there, but the cameras didn't capture them anywhere."

"I saw them too," says Crude. "As clearly as I see you now. Tall, skinny dudes with skin darker than mine. They had dog faces with a long muzzle, ugly as sin."

"Anubis," Yarza pronounces, "God of the necropolis."

"Well, we played the whole recording and the cameras didn't catch a soul," says Patch.

"Are you calling me a liar?" challenges Crude.

"Silence, everyone! I've got enough shit in my head without listening to you idiots arguing. Aborigine, activate the emergency radio beacon."

"Radio beacon activated, Captain."

"Tell me something good, Aborigine."

"Sorry, Captain. I'm going to have to add to the shit in your head."

"Go on."

"Channel 110 is automatic. It's activated by verbal authorisation. We've had it on the whole time. I just noticed when I activated the radio beacon. I've just shut it down."

"Do you mean to tell me they've been listening to everything we've been saying?"

"Well, they could have heard everything. And if I were on the other end of the line, I'd also be able to track the video and download it."

"Fuck me. This is going to be a pretty dance."

"Do you know the one about the party, where the hostess tells two of the guests to ask a friend to dance?"

"No Doc, we don't. Give it your best shot," says Patch.

"Well, it turns out that her friend was uglier than the things Crude says he saw in that little floating mortuary over there, so the two guests start to argue. 'You take her out on the dance floor,' says one. 'No, you take her out,' replies the other. 'No, it's better if you take her.' 'No way, you take her out there.' They're still arguing when along comes another guest, drunk out of his gourd, and gets involved in the discussion. 'Whas the problem, you shickens? All thish you take her out, no you, no you. Wash how I take her out, learn from a pro.' So he starts yelling, 'Hey, you, ugly bish! Open that door and get out or I'll take you out!'"

"Don't overdo it, Doc. The oven's not hot enough already?" says Drill.

"Why was the baker in a panic? He was in a loaf or death situation."

"Don't strain yourself. Really."

3

Space Monitoring Centre
Houston
Local Time: 01.10

Colonel Benson has been asleep for fifteen minutes when the phone rings. He came to the control room at quarter past twelve completely exhausted, having persuaded his team they needed to rest a while. After reluctantly dragging themselves away from the monitors, the men ate one of those one-dollar sandwiches dispensed from the blue machine in corridor four, took a shower to try and forget the awful taste of the food and went to bed in one of the bunks on the third floor underground, resolved to sleep until five. But it wasn't five o'clock. Colonel Benson checks his watch again: ten past one! He picks up the phone.

"This had better be something serious," he grumbles.

"Sorry to wake you, sir. We've got news."

"Who is this?"

"Private second Jeremy Epson, sir. I stayed on watch in the control room, sir."

"What's the news?"

"There are no longer two echoes, sir. There's only one."

"Son, I'm glad you take your work so seriously, but that's irrelevant. It just means the *Antipodes* has tethered the intruder and is bringing it home."

"That explanation can't be right, sir. The echo measures five kilometres and is approaching us at almost a million kilometres per hour. The cargo vessel *Antipodes* has four two-megawatt Samsung S-4 engines. They can't go that fast, sir."

Almost a million. A million! I was so happy dreaming. I was in a changing room full of girls, like that afternoon. It even seemed like the same training session, the same changing room, the same girls, only this time, instead of pinching me to death and throwing me naked into the hallway, they were kissing me and inviting me into the shower.

"Good work, Private."

"Thank you, sir."

"Wake everyone up. And get them to turn on the runway lights."

"Should I wake Mr Fischer up too, sir?"

"I don't think that'll be necessary. He's probably tapped my phone."

They hear a distant chuckle and a faint voice says, "No, you don't need to wake me up. I guess you know all the tricks, right Benson?"

"That's what they pay me for, sir."

Before the clock strikes a quarter to two, everyone is at their post, trying to rouse themselves with hot coffee. Fischer is there too, standing beside Benson, seemingly unperturbed that he does not even reach the colonel's shoulder.

"So?" Benson asks David Hooper.

"The only reasonable conclusion is that the intruder has released an anti-friction balloon before initiating the acceleration. The *Antipodes* has either disintegrated or they've trapped it inside the balloon. I'd prefer to believe the latter."

"That's very interesting, Hooper, but way off base. They can't have any friction without an atmosphere. An anti-friction balloon makes no sense in empty space. They've still a good way to go until they reach Mars's orbit. What friction might be there, Hooper?"

"They're Sorensen's calculations, sir."

"Go ahead, Sorensen, surprise us."

"Even in a vacuum, the friction experienced by a vessel depends on its speed, on its prow's engagement surface, whether it rotates or not and at what angle. There are very few atoms in empty space, mainly hydrogen and helium, but if you reach a sufficient velocity, it's like going up against a brick wall. Do you remember the ramjet project designed by Bussard in 1960? The project was useless because..."

Benson slams his fist on the desk, "Get to the point, Sorensen!"

"The size of the protective balloon along with its approximate geometry deduced from the time difference between the different radar detection systems allow us to calculate the level of friction estimated by the intruder's designers. If we know that friction level and we know the density of the space they have to travel through, we can calculate the velocity they plan to reach and the necessary acceleration. The intruder doesn't seem to respect any of our spiral trajectories and it doesn't look like they're going to respect the limitations of Hohmann's orbital calculations, but we can deduce the highest probability for the booster vectors and use them..."

"TO THE POINT!"

"The intruder is still accelerating. Right now, its velocity is nearly one and a half million kilometres per hour. It will leave Mars's orbit in six hours and it will get here before Tuesday. With our propulsion systems, that would be impossible, but with theirs..."

There are a few seconds of silence. Only a hum can be heard, perhaps the air conditioning.

"I must inform the President," murmurs Fischer, talking more to himself than to those present.

"I get the feeling we haven't managed to surprise you, Mr Fischer."

Fischer observes Benson with a fatigued air.

"Sirs," says Benjamin Fischer, "you are doing a great job. I think you deserve to know the whole truth, though I must warn you that you are forbidden from telling anyone. If the information I'm going to share with you gets out, you will be accused of high treason. Understood?"

"Perfectly, sir," says Benson and his team nod in agreement.

"When Captain Tanner activated channel 110, I started up my own electronic equipment. It's a remote system. It's not here physically, but it's very efficient."

"Do you mean to say you've received something through channel 110? On the main panel it says 'Pending activation.'"

"I apologise. I succumbed to the temptation of concealing all this, but I think you deserve to know it. Let's start with the audio. Listen to this."

"Woohoo! Yeeeaaah! We're rich, guys!"

"Aborigine, Doc, Tripod, Professor, you want to tell me what's going on?"

"What about Drill and Crude? Where are they?"

"That thing swallowed them."

...

"Silence, everyone! I've got enough shit in my head without listening to you idiots arguing. Aborigine, activate the emergency radio beacon."

"Radio beacon activated, Captain."

"Tell me something good, Aborigine."

"Now watch this video. It was recorded on Mike Gould's, the mechanic's camera," says Fischer.

The image of the inside of the vessel, immense and dark, stuns everyone. The aligned boxes that look like coffins half-illuminated in the reddish light only inspires fear. The recording ends, leaving everyone dumbstruck. Hooper breaks the silence.

"With all this information," he says, "what we can do is christen the intruder. Any god from the Egyptian pantheon will do. How about *Horus*?"

Nobody answers. The name doesn't seem to matter to them.

"Sir."

"Yes, Sorensen."

"We haven't talked about the glow."

"The glow? What glow? It's too small to see the solar reflection from here."

"I'm not talking about solar reflection, sir. Friction heats things. And the engines produce heat too, whatever they're burning. The radars indicate that right now the intruder is projecting a vapour trail five hundred kilometres long, which seems to be water. Because of its interaction with the solar wind, we know that it's travelling surrounded by a very powerful magnetic field, which has already created an effect similar to the aurora borealis. We need to find out lots more details, but the thermodynamics are relentless. It should start to glow at some point."

"Oh my God, have you been able to calculate the magnitude of the glow?"

"I'm afraid so. We don't have all the details: fuel, the nature of the protective membrane, the exact field value... That means there's a huge margin of error. But we can affirm that within twelve hours it'll be visible with a simple pair of binoculars."

"It'll be daytime. How long can we keep this a secret?"

"Yes, it will be daytime, but there's absolutely no chance of keeping it secret, sir. Today it will be little more than a small blue dot, but by tomorrow nobody will be talking about anything else. Half the world's population will spend the night watching it, pointing at it and sharing homemade telescopes while the other half will spend the day glued to the news channels."

"Half the world will go crazy," comments Kramer, a

specialist in database coordination. "And the other half already has been for some time."

"How am I supposed to deliver this kind of news to the President?" wonders Fischer.

"I'd give it to him straight, no beating around the bush," says Benson. "Anyway, whatever way you tell him, the only thing you can be sure of is that he's going to flip out."

"Can we at least keep what we know about the inside a secret? You know, the whole coffin-like boxes thing?"

"No way," says Hooper. "That video will be doing the rounds on the social networks before you've decided to wake the President."

"That's where you're wrong. I'm going to wake him up right now. And if there's no alternative, we'll shut down the Internet."

"Now you're the one who's mistaken, Mr Fischer. All the networks are triplicated or quadrupled. If the American servers collapse, the ones in the Philippines will still be working. And if those collapse, there's the European circuit and the submarine repeaters. Or the biochip network they've set up in Taipei. Whatever you do, the Internet will still work and people will still send messages. And you can bet your bottom dollar that within two days every message will be talking about the same thing: the end of the world and Revelation. What's more they'll be talking about the one hundred and forty thousand Revelation says will be saved, identified by a seal on their foreheads, while the rest of mankind burns."

"I can just imagine the rest. People will do anything to their foreheads: cuts, burns, whatever they can think of," says Fischer dismally.

"Tattoo artists will make a fortune," adds Benson.

Benjamin Fischer moves a hand to his mouth. He doesn't press anything; he's only wearing a discreet gold ring. He just says, "Call the President." There is a moment of silence.

"Mr President."

"..."

"Yes, I know it's very late, but I have to tell you something of the utmost gravity."

"..."

"The Secretary gave me very precise orders about it: my priority is to inform you. Plus, I have been told his wife's condition has worsened. Perhaps it would be best to leave her in New York for a few days."

"..."

"Have no concerns on that front, sir. I can assure you that Colonel Benson's team are up to the task. They're all very good, starting with Benson himself."

"..."

"Yes, sir, they know as much as I do. I think they deserve to, sir."

"..."

"They know how to keep their mouths shut, I give you my word."

"..."

"If you'll allow me to use a metaphor, sir, we've got two days until the Apocalypse."

"..."

"If you don't mind me saying so, sir, you should be on your way to Mount Weather right now. Your personal safety is of paramount importance."

"..."

"Understood, Mr President. It will be an honour."

Benjamin Fischer says, "End call."

Now they have seem him use it, it is evident he has a phone implanted in the ring, but nobody could have suspected it. Fischer looks around at Benson and his team. He gaze rests with particular intensity on David Hooper's tie, which seems to become even more grotesque the more he looks at it.

"Colonel. Gentlemen. I'm going to have to give you a crash course in protocol. The President is ignoring my advice to take shelter in the underground facilities at Mount Weather. He's coming here instead."

HORUS

4

Aboard the Cargo Spaceship Antipodes
Time on the spacecraft: 01.45

"How are the headaches, guys?" asks Doc.

Everyone is on the command deck strapped to their backrests and with a belly full of painkillers. Nobody wanted to go to their bunk; they feel more secure staying together.

"Great, thanks. I can hardly feel it. My stomachache is so bad I can't think about anything else, not even the fact my head is exploding. My dad warned me. He said, 'The further away from home a man is, the worse things get.' Well, there you go. To Mars and beyond."

"You're a complainer, Drill, a midget whiner who doesn't know how to shut his mouth."

"When I can stand up, Tripod, I'm going to show you what a right hook looks like."

"Our heads hurt too," says Captain Tanner, "so give it a rest, both of you. Aborigine, any news?"

Johnny Wash has put his backrest down as far as it goes and is lying down with a Lakers cap over his eyes. It has been a while since he has had anything to do because all the tracking, measuring and calculating systems are down. He feels as if his head is going to burst open as well. It is as though someone were inflating a hot air balloon inside his skull. He has just taken his fourth painkiller.

"Nothing, Captain. According to my latest calculations, we'll reach Earth on Monday, arriving around five in the morning, Houston time. If we park in front of the house, we can ask them in for breakfast."

"Assuming we're still alive," says Yarza.

"That's right, you stay optimistic," says Patch.

"How did you calculate the braking time?" wonders Doc.

"Ask me when my headache's gone."

"I think I'm gonna throw up."

"Don't you dare, Drill," says Tripod.

5

Space Monitoring Centre
Houston
Local Time: 03.00

Colonel Benson is standing to attention and the men in his team have adopted a feeble imitation of his stance. Benjamin Fischer enters the room with three generals: Brown, Bowers and Simmons. None of them has space for any more medals on their chests, although they seem to be a little old for earning too many more. Fischer makes the introductions. Then four soldiers as voluminous as Benson but with a level of fitness he has not experienced for years enter wearing camouflage and green berets embroidered with a yellow knife. Each of them goes to stand in one of the four corners of the room. Their task is evident. They are immediately followed by the fiftieth president of the United States, Republican Harry Spencer Grant, as elegant as ever despite only having slept for an hour and a half.

"Mr President, allow me to introduce you to Colonel Benson."

"It's an honour to meet you, Mr President."

"And his team, Zimmerman, Kramer, Stephenson, McBride, Hooper and Sorensen."

"Sir."

"You've done a fine job, I'm grateful to you. Do you have any further news?"

"Go ahead, Sorensen. And no dancing around the

houses."

"The intruder will reach Earth on Monday, sir. We don't know what kind of braking system it will use, but if it wants to land on our planet, my calculations tell me it could land around zero five hundred hours, Houston time."

"What do we know about the *Antipodes*? Has it appeared on the screen again?"

"Your turn, Hooper," instructs Benson.

"No, sir. We haven't been able to establish any further contact whatsoever with the cargo vessel."

"In that case, we must assume the intruder is hostile. The first thing it did was to destroy one of our spacecraft. And, unless God Himself has intervened, they've killed its entire crew."

"Hooper!" yells Benson. "Can you behave appropriately in front of the President, for God's sake!"

Hooper has sat down in front of his terminal and is activating a blue grid in which a yellow trajectory and five green lights are glowing.

"Sir, I think the *Antipodes* is still in one piece. Look at this. Our trackers don't seem to detect anything, but that's because they're programmed to search for a series of preset frequencies. I've run the range of sample frequencies in blue and look at the result: these green dots represent the *Antipodes*' automatic radio beacon emissions."

"Why aren't they being emitted in the preset frequency?"

"They are, but they're affected by the intruder's

velocity, which is close to three million kilometres per hour. I think the intruder is carrying the *Antipodes* in its thermal protection balloon. The emissions are distorted by a large magnetic field and affected by such a large Doppler effect that our instruments perceive it as out of range and can't compensate for it. But I'm convinced that these signals are the hourly emissions from the cargo ship's emergency radio beacons. In fact, on the audio recording, the last thing we heard was the order to activate the beacon. So, the intruder is towing the cargo ship in one piece. And, for now, the most logical conclusion is that there's no reason to suppose the crew is dead or to assume the intruder is hostile. I wouldn't even call it an intruder. I would call it a visitor."

Benson clears his throat.

"Sir!" adds Hooper.

"So you're David Hooper. I've heard a lot about you in the past few hours. I see you are a man with your own ideas. And initiative. Do you think there's any chance of keeping this secret, Doctor Hooper?"

"Impossible. Even if it doesn't start to glow, the astronomical observatories will detect its presence. At this point, they are probably calling each other already to compare coordinates. Plus, there's something else we haven't mentioned: the only visible planet is Mars, and that's only at twilight. The others are in conjunction. I don't know whether it's a coincidence or not, but the sky is very clear; it's as if the intruder wanted to be highly visible."

The President sits down next to Hooper in Zimmerman's chair and asks for a coffee. He flinches a little on seeing Hooper's tie up close, but manages to disguise his aversion quite well.

"So, no secrets. Well then. Colonel Benson, give us your opinion. What is this thing flying towards Earth?"

"I have no idea, sir. But I can't forget my military training: I would have everybody on maximum alert with their weapons fully loaded and the safety off for when it arrives. Just in case."

"You're my kind of guy, Benson. But if we put the armed forces on maximum alert..."

"We increase the chances that civilians will know something strange is afoot and we'll be closer to chaos," interrupts Hooper.

Benson clears his throat again. "Sir!" he says to Hooper.

"Correct, Hooper." The President does not raise his voice when he says, "General Brown."

"Sir!"

"Put the Air Force on Defcon 3."

"Yes, sir." General Brown leaves the room.

"Defcon 3, sir?"

"Don't worry, Hooper, it won't affect the general population. Only those who are at an airport. Mr Fischer."

"Sir."

"Call my three close buddies again, Takeshi Yamamoto, Ekaterina Chernenko and Heinrich Berlinger. What a trio! I wouldn't even lend them a biro, but I suppose we must get along with them. You know what you have to say to them. And get word out that we're going to issue a joint statement to the whole of mankind. Make it sound like a peaceful rumour, like we're going to give the world some good news."

6

Director J. J. Bradley's Office
Daily Morning Newsroom
Houston
Local Time: 07.00

"Sit down, Mary."

"Thanks."

"It's been a while since you've been in the newsroom."

"Yeah, I don't come here much in person."

"Now then, I know we haven't given you much except lightweight stuff lately. I also know how badly we've been paying you. But today is different. This is no bullshit story and we're not talking about chump change either."

"What are we talking then, a couple of million?"

"Who knows? Do you know who Benjamin Fischer is?"

"The name rings a bell. Defence Department?"

"Bingo. Benjamin Fischer is the Secretary of Defence's right-hand man. And do you know where he was yesterday?"

"At the Space Monitoring Centre."

"How the hell... How did you know that?"

"You asked me if I liked astronomy, remember? So I put two and two together."

"Smart girl. It's a waste of your talent having you filling out the last few minutes."

"If you want to appoint me assistant director, I accept."

"You never know. Right, let's get to the point. Yesterday lunchtime something very serious happened at the Space Centre. Around twelve-thirty p.m., when most normal people are eating their lunch, Colonel Benson called the Secretary of Defence's office. I can't access the content of the conversation, even though I gave a good wodge of dough to the IT team. Anyway, we don't know exactly what Benson said, but we do know that Benjamin Fischer left Washington at around three p.m. and that he was talking to Benson and his team in person by around six."

"How do you know all this?"

"Bribes. I pay nearly all the security guards you can think of: at the airport, the Space Centre, the nuthouse, you name it. Security guards are the first to find out who's coming and going. So, the thing is that they were waiting for Benjamin Fischer on the runway with one of those gismos the Germans have invented, a plasma transporter, one of those whatchamacallits..."

"A Holstein?"

"That's it, a Holstein. The rest of us keep on driving around in tins on four wheels like it was the Stone Age, but Mr Fischer gets a Holstein with an automatic sequencer, you know? From the airport to the Space Centre in under ten minutes. Something serious must be going on. Rumour has it it's a meteorite. A great big meteorite that's headed straight for us, like the one that brushed past our atmosphere last year, remember?"

"Of course I remember. The Apofis meteorite."

"Right, how could you forget the fuss that thing created?"

"And why have you called me?"

"Number one rule of journalism: take advantage of all your resources."

"Resources?"

"Yeah. And this time we have the biggest advantage of all: we've got someone on the inside."

"Me?"

"Yep, you. You know one of Benson's team."

"Seriously?"

"David Hooper. Doctor David Hooper. Mathematician."

"David Hooper? A doctor in mathematics? Good Lord, the last time I saw him he was about twelve or thirteen years old. He was a really nice boy, quite good looking and skinnier than a string bean. So, he's a mathematician working at the Space Centre, is he? And you want me to go and talk to him? He'll never remember me. It's been twelve years."

"Oh, he'll remember you all right."

"Oh, and why is that?"

"I swear I'd remember. Your mom worked for the Hoopers, didn't she? Cleaning, ironing, and so on?"

"Cooking, mostly cooking. She made desserts that could win awards."

"And you went to help your mom from time to time?"

"Yes. I helped out in the kitchen or with the ironing."

"And you were what, nineteen or thereabouts? And Hooper was thirteen or fourteen. Do you see where I'm going with this?"

"No, not in the slightest."

"You've just turned thirty-two. Happy birthday, by the way."

"Thanks."

"When you came to the newsroom you were twenty-four. Now you're a very beautiful woman, Mary. When you joined the team, you were Miss World."

"That's very kind of you to say so. Where's the catch?"

"There's no catch, Mary, no catch. I'm just trying to make you understand that when have an ace up your sleeve you have to play your cards. When Hooper was thirteen a gorgeous nineteen-year-old was wandering around his house in the afternoons helping to prepare his supper. And you don't think he'll remember you? I bet my dog he will. He'll have had you in his bedtime prayers many a time. Call him. Meet up with him. Get everything he knows out of him."

"But... I don't know if..."

"Benjamin Fischer wouldn't have come in person just because of a simple meteorite. He wouldn't have come in person even if the moon disappeared from the sky. If he has come in person, my dear Mary, it must be something truly momentous, something worth being on the front line for. Something that might deserve a special edition, one of those editions nostalgic people ask us to print on paper, on smudged cellulose with real black ink, even if we have to charge them a fortune for each issue. So I want you to put on a pretty skirt and a low-cut blouse, call Hooper and get him to tell you everything he knows whichever way you can."

"Are you suggesting...?"

"That you sleep with Hooper a couple of times if need be? Yes, that's what I'm suggesting. And that you get us a major scoop. Because behind this visit from one of Washington's little fish is a big story. And I want it for tomorrow's edition. So you've got today to make this boy's prayers come true. Listen—and stop making faces—I didn't make the world the way it is and it's not my fault that two nice legs are worth more than one good case file. If you'd put your scruples in a bag the moment you left college, you'd have a Pulitzer Prize by now. But you've spent seven years being a Poor Clare nun and look where it's gotten you. Is that clear?"

"As day."

"Opportunity is knocking at your door, Mary. It won't stand around waiting for you all day; it doesn't like waiting. And, do you know what the worst thing about opportunity is? When the last chance arrives, you don't know it *is* the last chance. If you let this one go, if you let it walk off your porch and march off into the sunset, you'll never know whether that knock will come again. By the way, didn't you say that this Hooper kid was a nice guy and pretty handsome?"

"Yes, very nice, always in a good mood. A real charmer, not..."

"Go on, say it, don't stop there: 'A real charmer, not like you'."

"I wasn't thinking that exactly."

"But something along those lines. Well, I didn't write the rulebook, you know? Look on the bright side: if he was a bitter, ugly guy it would be more difficult to pretend you wanted to raise his antennae."

"Save the jokes, boss. You know that I'm five or six years older than him, right?"

"What does that matter, hey? What does that matter? Since when has age been an issue? The best sex I ever had in my life was in the last year of high school and it wasn't exactly with someone my own age. It was with my history teacher! I was eighteen; she was over forty. Her husband had gone to buy cigarettes a few months earlier and never come back and it seems that at some point during the graduation ceremony she decided it was time to get back in the game. She began by drinking ten glasses of punch and ended up choosing me to play a game of two halves with extra time. That reminds me, I haven't offered you a drink."

"It's a little early for me."

"Coffee?"

"Coffee, yes. It might help me organise my thoughts a little."

"Great, a positive attitude. By the way, just to cover all the bases, if you want to rehearse with me before you meet Hooper..."

"What if I say yes and your blood pressure shoots up?"

James Bradley falls silent and sits very still, lost in thought. He gives the impression of someone who has just received bad news by means of telepathy. He normally walks very upright, like a soldier on parade, but now he suddenly seems deflated. When he speaks again, his voice has clearly lost its boom.

"Truth be told, I don't know how I can joke like this when I know my heart can only take a couple more scares."

"Don't go down that road, boss, you can't soften me up like that."

"I'm not trying to, I'm serious this time. I'm going to let you in on a secret: I've only got six or seven months left to live. I'm not going to make it to my fifty-fifth birthday. Careful with the cup, it's hot. That's it, leave it there. I won't see two more Christmases, one if I'm lucky. Seven months from now I'll be looking at my last twinkling lights on the tree, hanging my last stocking on the fireplace, eating my last stuffed turkey. I've spent my life filling my lungs with smoke and now it's time to pay the price. Mary, I swear that before I go I want to publish a great article written by you, a real story, a genuine scoop. A dazzling piece that will open the doors for you at the *New York Times* or the *Washington Post* or one of the other big guns, the *Herald Tribune*, the *Berliner Zeitung*, the *Pravda*... It's okay, don't get all worked up because I'm shedding a couple of tears. After all, I've got plenty to cry about. I've messed up a bunch of things, Mary, a whole big bunch. I thought the time to set things right was as far off as the day the Houston Rockets win the league. But my time is up, just around the corner. And in the final reckoning there's something I'm truly ashamed of and that's having put you to one side and not given you the job you deserve. I've been petty. Maybe if I say it out loud, the judgment that awaits me will be a little less severe. I know there are others who could wheedle their way into the Space Centre to find out what's going on and what Fischer is poking around for, dig up why they've photoshopped the images available on all the astronomy websites, as if something really ugly were flying towards us, but I want you to do it. Mary, this is not your last chance for success, but it might just be my last shot at redemption."

"James?"

"What?"

"I do want you to invite me out for dinner tonight."

"No way. I'm not worth it anymore."

7

Cairo
Local Time: 07.30

"Welcome to Cairo," says Nancy Howard. "You're going to love it."

I doubt that, thinks her brother. Accustomed as he was to the chilly Scottish climate with its perpetual wetness and timid sun, which could go months without peeking out from behind the clouds, venturing into the burning heat of the Egyptian desert did not seem such a good idea. His shirt clung to his skin with sweat, his hair was gritty with sand and the inside of his nostrils felt as though they had been flayed.

I've just got here and I'm already regretting it.

"Cairo owes its present name to a phonetic disfiguration. In the Arabic language," Doctor Mathias Shepard explains, "this fascinating city has a woman's name: Al-Qéhira, 'the triumphant one'."

To Ted Howard's way of thinking, the competitions in which Cairo could triumph didn't warrant a mention: noisiest city in the world, worst smelling city, dustiest city.

Certainly nothing to boast about.

"Well, I don't see the charm in this hotchpotch of old houses," he says to his companions as he swats a large, olive green mosquito away from his face.

"You will see it, I guarantee it. Cairo initially repulses but ends up seducing. We have all been through the same process. At first all one sees are the negatives: the incessant hustle and bustle, the maddening noise, the dust from the desert, the impoverished quarters, the swarm of animals... But then suddenly one day, when you least expect it, you discover a spot in this unfathomable maze that you wish to claim as your own for eternity. Mine is on the banks of the Nile, very near the new Coptic cemetery. Some day I would like my bones to rest there."

"I know, Professor," interrupts Nancy. "You've told me many a time. I know where I have to bury you if you go first."

"Of course I shall go first, my dear. To go second would be a discourtesy for which I could never forgive myself. I shall go first, naturally. Here, in Cairo, cradled by the waters of the Nile. Although, upon reflection, my bones would like to be anywhere, as long as they are in Egypt. Would you mind terribly if I allowed myself the impertinence of asking where you would like to be buried, Doctor Howard."

"I spent my childhood patrolling Loch Ness. The conviction that a family of plesiosaurs lived there was what first converted me into a biologist; I was a palaeontologist for a while and then finally a geneticist," Ted replies.

"Do you mean to say you would like to be buried near Loch Ness? You will have to be more specific: Loch Ness covers several square miles."

"What I'd like is to be thrown in the loch. If at all possible in the middle of winter, during a snowstorm. They'd have to break the ice to lob me in the water."

"You never told me that," says his sister.

"Nobody's ever asked me."

"Best not ask me, you'll think I'm completely mad," says Nancy.

"Why?" asks Ted.

"Because I have a recurring dream where I'm buried on another planet, a really long way from Earth. Little skinny men with dark skin bury me."

"You never told me that."

"You never asked. Right, that's enough chitchat. This is our hotel."

Ted has come to Cairo with hopes of staying in the Semiramis InterContinental or the Ramses Hilton, but the university budget has not stretched quite that far. However, nor are they staying in student residences at the University of Cairo, next to the Gizah District. Instead they leave their luggage in the Red Pyramid, an average hotel with fifty rooms and acceptable cleaning standards for European guests, located midway between the new Spanish Embassy and the Museum of Antiquities. It faces the botanical garden on Gezira Island, which has been impeccably restored after a fire.

In the entrance lobby, everyone is talking about a rumour saying that the President of the United States is about to issue a statement. Some are adding that the statement will be made jointly by the four major leaders: the American, the Russian, the Japanese and the European heads of state or union. There has been some mention of an extraterrestrial spaceship but, even though it was the President who was due to announce the discovery, they did not pay much heed. They had work to do and would think about aliens later on. Besides, after a few days they would probably prove that the spacecraft was Russian, Japanese or German or something. Or even American. Either way, the way history had dealt the cards was disheartening. There were now four main powers: America, with the unpredictable Harry Grant in the White House; Europe, led from Berlin by the financial genius Heinrich Berlinger; Russia, the capital of which had a population of three hundred million, the most congested on the planet; and Japan, with its unrivalled exporting power thanks to the fact it had all but annexed China. It seemed strange that the Chinese leader Li Yuan-Chi had accepted Takeshi Yamamoto's leadership, but people always end up capitulating in the face of profitable results. Meanwhile, the United Kingdom was on the fringes of the four superpowers, isolated, marginalised and self-involved. Professor Shepard, an expert in ancient history, liked to say that the splendid period of the British Empire now formed part of his specialist subject. He sometimes added that the growing friendship between Yamamoto and Berlinger disturbed him, to which people usually replied that he should stick to the Egyptians.

The rooms for the three academics are on the sixth floor. They go up in a fascinating type of lift: a wooden cubicle that closes with a double metal door and has buttons with numbers on a panel to one side. To reach the sixth floor they have to press the button marked '6'. With their finger! They have to press it with their finger! The lift must have been installed when Napoleon visited the pyramids.

On the sixth floor there is a large window facing southeast. In the distance, shimmering in the desert heat, are the profiles of three mountainous peaks.

"I didn't know there were mountains in Egypt," says Ted. "I thought it was completely flat."

Nancy Howard and Mathias Shepard chuckle. Nancy approaches her brother and puts an arm around his shoulders.

"Impressive, aren't they? I've been here thirty times and they still amaze me."

"You mean...? Are you trying to tell me those three mountains are the pyramids?"

"That's Menkaure on the left, Khefre is in the middle and Khufu's pyramid is on the right. They rest on a raised plateau while Cairo is built at sea level, which increases the optical effect."

"How far away are they?"

"The road to Giza is eight kilometres long, so they must be about nine from here."

"God, they must be absolutely massive!"

"Wait till you see them up close."

"When can we go?"

"Right now, as soon as we change our clothes. You won't want to go looking like that."

After putting on outfits the same colour as the desert sand, boots and hat included, they climb onto the magnetic carriageway that runs parallel to the ancient road to Giza. It was designed to transport the five hundred people who travelled to the pyramids each hour without them making any effort or breaking a sweat. Curiously enough, there was always somebody who preferred to walk, perspiring as if they were in a sauna and taking over two hours to get there instead of the quarter of an hour the magnetic carriageway took. Those who journeyed along the ancient road on foot said that seeing how the pyramids grew before their very eyes with each step on the two-hour journey until they filled the sky was so intense that everyone in the world should experience it at least once in their life. It was like followers of Islam recommending fellow Muslims to go on the pilgrimage to Mecca.

The trio circumvent the tourist area and go directly to the excavation zone. The shouts are deafening. People are running around in no particular direction as if they have lost their minds, hugging and yelling each other like footballers who have just won the final. Amidst the hubbub they discern one word uttered repeatedly: "Jufu, jufu, jufu."

"Is the local football team called Jufu?" asks Ted. "Sounds like they've won the cup final, doesn't it?"

His sister fails to answer; she is even paler than normal. Doctor Shepard shakes his head.

"No, my friend, far from it. Jufu is the Egyptian pronunciation for the pharaoh who ordered the construction of the Great Pyramid: Khufu."

"So why are they all yelling his name?"

"It would appear they have found his tomb."

8

Space Monitoring Centre
Houston
Local Time: 09.00

Mary Sanchez walks back home in the hope that the fresh morning air will help her come to a decision. First she feeds her cats and then, after taking three deep breaths and downing a shot of mescal, she tries to contact David Hooper. However, it seems that Doctor Hooper has disappeared off the face of the earth. He is not answering any calls, he is not connected to the Internet and he is not responding to any of her text messages. Nothing, zip, nada.

She checks the websites dedicated to showing views of the sky and, just as her boss had intimated, some are blocked while others only show images taken several days earlier. As for the fact that James Bradley is dying of lung cancer, all she wants is to drive that thought out of her mind.

Mary calls the Space Centre and a pleasant voice politely informs her that nobody who works there is available to talk to anyone, least of all the press, as they are all completely tied up with a serious IT breakdown. "Thank you for your understanding. Have a nice day."

She rummages around in her wardrobe until she finds her blond wig.

"Ah-ha! There you are! That's everything I need."

Taking State Highway 4, Mary heads to the Space Centre. A voice in her head is warning her she is about to get herself into a heap of trouble, but another voice is telling her opportunities don't wait around on the porch all day long. She decides to listen to the latter.

Stick your scruples in a bag and toss them in the sea.

She reaches the turn off at ten on the dot but drives past it. She does not want to go to the main entrance, she wants to see the car park. Sure enough there are a good number of vehicles with government licence plates. Too many.

And two of those German gizmos, what are they called? Holsteins, two Holsteins. They say they cost a fortune. Right, scruples out the window.

Mary enters the public car park, where the ticket booths are open and the Space Centre guides are assisting visitors. As often happens, to disguise the fact that something serious is happening everything seems to be business as usual. She buys a ticket, follows the signs and listens to the guide before feigning interest in a replica of the Saturn rocket and slipping away to the toilets. After switching her reversible skirt and jacket around, Mary cleans off her make-up and puts on a much paler version. She lightens her eyebrows, puts her hair up in a bun and dons the blond wig. Finally, she pins a name card onto her jacket. From a brown-haired woman dressed in black she has turned into a blond stewardess called Hannah wearing a white and blue uniform. It looks like a good disguise to her as she takes one last look in the mirror and adjusts the wig before stepping back out into the corridor.

Three minutes later she is being held by the security guards. All her doubts vanish: something really big is going on! Her captors are not your run-of-the-mill security guards. These guys are in great physical shape and carry weapons Mary has never seen before. In less time than it had taken her to put on her disguise, they have searched her from head to toe, with no eye contact whatsoever.

Before she has time to think, she is sitting in an interrogation room flanked by two guards wearing expressions that suggest they would not know how to find the word 'friendly' in the dictionary. Opposite her sits a man straight out of a spy film: impeccable black suit, dark glasses and a face as expressionless as a statue of a fish.

He does not bother to ask for any identification, he merely focuses a type of laser beam on her and immediately starts reading from a screen.

"Mary Sanchez. Born in Mexico. Journalist. Is that correct?"

"Yes."

"Today is May fourth. It's not Halloween."

"No, sir." Mary feels increasingly unnerved. "It's not Halloween."

"Do you want to give me some kind of explanation?"

"I though it was a good idea... and... I need to speak to Doctor David Hooper. I tried calling him several times... I'm worried. Do you know if something has happened to him?"

"I meant a coherent explanation."

Throw your fear into the sea. You're a journalist. You have rights.

"I know that Benjamin Fischer is here. I'm a journalist. I've come to ask for an interview with him."

"Of course! I hope you are comfortable in this room."

The man leaves the room and locks it. He takes over half an hour to return.

"Take off that ridiculous disguise, fix yourself up a bit and come with me."

"I have to fix myself up? What, am I going to meet Benjamin Fischer in person?"

"You are going to meet Harry Grant, the President of the United States."

"The President, no less. I'll believe it when I see it."

They go down three floors. A soldier is posted at each door. They walk along a corridor, go down in a lift and then climb up three flights of stairs.

This is unbelievable. They're trying to disorientate me.

They reach the Space Centre's monitoring room. The President offers his hand.

"Ms Sanchez."

"Mr President." Mary manages to make her voice sound almost normal. "It is an honour, sir."

She is introduced to a plethora of people and only manages to retain the surnames Simmons, Benson, Kramer, Sorensen and Zimmerman. She glances sideways at Hooper, hardly recognising him. If it were not for the hideous tie he was wearing, he would be incredibly attractive.

The President reads something on a small screen he holds in his hand.

"Well, well, well. So you work for J. J. Bradley. He must be, what, fifty-five? Do you know how he's survived for so long?"

"Sorry, I don't understand the question."

"Because he came to live in Houston. Far from the world of politics. If he'd stayed in Washington, he would've had an accident a long time ago. What a guy. He liked to meddle in places he shouldn't. Are you some kind of advance party? No, no, you don't have to answer that. Just tell me how J. J. knew Mr Fischer was here."

"I cannot answer that, Mr President."

"And why were you looking at astronomy websites before you came here?"

"I was told they aren't showing images in real time any more, like they usually do. People are starting to ask what they're trying to hide. A meteorite maybe?"

"There's already a rumour we're hiding something?"

"Yes, sir."

"So we're hiding the arrival of a meteorite?"

"That's what lots of people who connect to these websites are starting to think."

"I wish we could make people think it was a meteorite."

"I beg your pardon, sir, what did you say?"

"It would be easier. 'Ladies and gentlemen, it is a

meteorite. Do not be afraid, it's just going to brush past us, like last year.' Unfortunately, the earth is teeming with amateur astronomers who can interpret the data correctly, so if I broadcast a message telling them this meteorite tale, after ten minutes thousands of astronomers would be calling my bluff and after fifteen minutes millions of people would know that I'm lying. And we all know that lies and politicians go hand in hand, of course we do, but it shouldn't be obvious. The question is how would people react?"

"I don't get where you're heading with this, sir."

"If I tell you the secret, I am condemning you to stay in these facilities until I personally give you permission to leave. Understood?"

"Yes, sir."

"What is approaching the earth is an extraterrestrial spacecraft nearly half a kilometre long. The conversations among the crew of the cargo spaceship *Antipodes*, who have boarded the strange vessel, are recorded by something similar to the black box on aircraft. According to the part of these conversations we've been able to recover, the spaceship has the same proportions as Noah's ark. What do you think so far?"

"Is it a joke?"

"Inside the spaceship are thousands of coffin-shaped boxes. Colonel Benson's team have calculated that within five hours there will be no way of keeping it a secret. An hour later half of humankind will know about it. And an hour after that even those four idiots from Denver who went to live in an igloo will know about it. You're a journalist, so tell me: how will people react?"

"I'm afraid…"

"Yes, I know. Total and utter chaos. But perhaps you being here is a good thing, you know? Many people distrust politicians. All politicians. They see our faces and automatically think, 'Don't believe half what this guy says.' But nobody will be looking at my face, they'll be looking at yours. Your face inspires confidence, Mary. Has anyone ever told you that? And when the curious investigate who you are, they'll find out you're the only child of some poor immigrants who, after being orphaned, worked really hard to graduate from journalism college and now has a social standing her parents never dreamed of, especially considering they were illegal immigrants. But you are a fine upstanding citizen, you have honoured your parents' memory. The American dream, Mary, you are the American dream."

"But…"

"There are no buts worth a damn. When I tell the world the news, you will be standing by my side. You're hired. Don't worry about your salary. Or your two cats."

"But…"

"Mr President," Benjamin Fischer intervenes, "this might be a hasty decision. Your press advisors should…"

"Don't bother, Fischer, the decision has been taken."

Born in Dallas to a multimillionaire family, Harry Grant inherited what were two of the greatest fortunes on the planet to date. He is not accustomed to being contradicted or given advice. He is a tall, dashing man with the unfortunate habit of looking at his adversaries with his eyelids half closed, making his eyes into two slits that heralded nothing positive. He sits down next to

Mary, revealing more of the black leather cowboy boots with a wooden heel, like the ones people wore two centuries ago, under his immaculately tailored suit. Whether this is to create a matching outfit or by way of contrast is unclear.

"Fischer doesn't understand, but I got to where I am today by trusting my gut instincts against all odds, so don't be nervous. Would you like a coffee, my dear?"

"Yes. Thanks," says Mary, aware that her voice is barely audible.

"Hey, Hooper. Stop hiding behind all those screens and come and give your friend a kiss hello before I do it for you."

David approaches the desk the President occupies and, smiling warmly, greets Mary with a phrase in Spanish that nobody else understands. Then he adds in English, "I haven't forgotten anything you taught me."

"It's great to see you again," says Mary, as she kisses him on the cheek.

They fall silent and gaze into one another's eyes, each of them trying to recognise the other after twelve years.

"That's a very promising start. I'm jealous, Hooper. Sit down next to me and explain where you got such a dreadful tie. I don't know which way to go: either I buy one myself to wear when I have to meet some Democratic congressman or I throw the guy who sold it to you in jail for an assault on public health."

"It didn't cost me a cent, sir. The Chinese guy who runs the store opposite the parking lot gives them away for free."

"For the love of God, Hooper," the President laughs heartily, "Now I know why I hate Li Yuan-Chi so much!"

Fischer grabs the chance to make peace with his boss by laughing at the joke.

"If you don't mind me asking," says Hooper, "how do you manage to stay so calm, Mr President?"

"In politics you learn the same as you do in war: if you get nervous, you're dead."

9

The Canary Islands
Local Time: 19.00

At the beginning of the century, social media networks became very famous. Those who are now combing the odd grey hair or those who are already dyeing theirs remember having used veritable relics such as Facebook, Twitter or Instagram with fondness. Now, in May 2030, every human being is connected to the Human network. If you send a private message (and the transmitters implanted in contact lenses, where a message is written simply by thinking it, are now old news), all the members of your personal network receive an alert at their leisure and they can see the message whenever and wherever they wish. Indeed, a large proportion of them receive the alert in the receivers incorporated in their contact lenses, despite the constant efforts by the heads of Highway Traffic to prohibit their use.

If you send a public message, in just a few hours it will have bounced around hundreds of associated subject channels so that all of humankind can potentially read it. With no language barriers. Even with seemingly complex pairs, such as Norwegian and Arabic, the automated translation tools achieve excellent results.

So everyone is interlinked, connected and networked, trapped for better or for worse in the invisible web. The antithesis of the shipwreck survivor. The last time someone checked the website "I too have managed to read *Robinson Crusoe*" there were still only forty-two followers and nobody else had signed up in eleven years.

Juan Exposito is no exception: he is connected to the great network too. He has not managed to read *Robinson Crusoe* either, even though he lives completely alone most of the time, five kilometres from the nearest town on a solitary hill on the island of Fuerteventura. Juan has been nocturnal for many years. While everyone else is asleep, he is awake with his eye glued to the telescope, enjoying the infinite spectacle the celestial dome offers to anyone who wants to watch it with virgin eyes.

All the astronomical observatories have spent several decades working with automated equipment while the astronomers sit facing virtual images, but Juan is old school. He loves to spend the night with his eye fixed on the lens of his Zeiss-Leica telescope, observing the rusty surface of Mars with a geologist's interest or the unsurpassable beauty of Jupiter's satellites with an artist's innocence.

In reality, even if there were more fans of optical telescopes in Europe, it would not make a difference. For the past two months Northern Europe has been darkened by the ash from an Icelandic volcano that seems to have gone mad resulting in extremely poor visibility from the Pyrenees to Ukraine. So Juan Exposito would still have been the first to realise that a new light was shining in the twilight, barely half an hour after sundown. Using maximum magnification along with green filters, the light reminds Juan of the tail of a comet. But the tail was not pointing away from the sun!

HORUS

Comprehension explodes in his brain: they are propulsion vapours with their own initial vector independent of the solar wind. So, as they extend, they curve. That glowing light is a spaceship! Juan tries to stay calm, cool-headed and impartial. But when he calculates that the object is nearly half a kilometre long his pulse shoots up past a hundred and forty. When he calculates that it is travelling at three million kilometres per hour, he tries to sit back down in his chair but instead falls to the floor. He pulls himself up and, with trembling hands and blood dripping from his nose, works out its approximate trajectory. The spaceship is situated very near the orbit of Mars, following an extremely eccentric and completely unnatural path. It is coming from a place that is impossible to divine with any precision towards the orbits of the interior planets. Juan feels dizzy and sits on the floor again, putting a piece of cotton wool up his nose.

Breathe deeply, breathe deeply. One, two, one, two. Easy, it's all right.

He calls the observatory but nobody picks up the phone. He gets up, leaves the house and starts running towards the garden. Managing to start up the engine on his skateboard, Juan speeds down towards the village as fast as he can without losing his balance.

When he gets there everyone is talking about the announcement. What announcement? The President's speech. What president? The President of the United States. What did he say? Nobody knows; there was just an alert that we all have to be on standby because he is going to say something very important to the whole of mankind. I know what he's going to tell us. Really? Yes, that an extraterrestrial spaceship is travelling towards

Earth. I've just seen it, that's why I came down here. A spaceship? Yes. Coming here? Yes. You saw a spaceship? Yes, I saw it. It's impossible to see it with the naked eye, but with the telescope you can see it perfectly.

Thirty-two people are listening to Juan Exposito. More than twenty of them go to their houses and return with binoculars or plastic telescopes. After ten minutes, the whole village has seen the tiny elongated white light travelling towards Earth.

By 8 p.m. local time in the Canary Islands, more than thirty million people have received the news via the Human network. At 8.30 p.m., 3.30 p.m. Houston time, President Harry Grant learns that half the world already knows about the approaching vessel. He can wait no longer. At 9 p.m. on the dot, Canary Islands time, a very beautiful woman, whose long black mane contrasts with the President's short blond hair and whose serene, luminous eyes contrast even more with Harry Grant's narrow slits, reads a statement on behalf of the four great leaders. "Citizens of Earth..."

The automated translation tools have been moving closer to perfection since 2018. Every individual on Earth, regardless of where they live, hears Mary Sanchez's voice speaking in their own language: in elegant, ceremonious Japanese; in faultless German; in exquisitely pronounced Russian. As if the Holy Spirit has returned to Earth in a new and unexpected Pentecost.

10

Cairo
Local Time: 22.00

"Try it, Ted," says Nancy Howard. "You'll like it."

"I doubt it. Since I've been in Egypt, I haven't liked a thing. Not even those sugary doughnut-like things," her brother replies.

"What about you, Professor, aren't you going to eat anything?"

"I don't know if my appetite shall ever return, my dear." The psychological blow has been immense. They gave the press conference to reveal the discovery of Khufu's tomb to an almost empty room. "Not in my worst nightmares could I have imagined something like this would happen."

"If we'd have spoken to the media at four o'clock this afternoon, we'd have been all right," says Nancy.

"I see what you mean," responds Professor Shepard. "By holding the press conference at half past eight, we were blindsided by that blessed announcement about an extraterrestrial spaceship, which will probably end up being a meteorite that will whizz past us without a second thought. But we must try and understand Doctor McCallum; put yourself in his shoes. As director of this excavation it was quite bold of him to call the press conference at half past eight. I would have required eight months rather than eight hours. You do realise we have demolished Egyptology, do you not? We have demonstrated that Ancient Egyptian history has to be completely rewritten: we have got nothing right. We cannot blame Doctor McCallum for needing eight hours to digest the magnitude of this find. What we should have done is told those journalists to get the hell out of Egypt."

"What time do restaurants normally close here?" asks Ted. "Maybe we should head back to the hotel."

"Let's order the last round of those wee mint cakes," Nancy counters.

"You have taken this very serenely, Doctor Howard. I must confess I am a little surprised."

"Och, it was easy for me to assimilate. I have always suspected that this would end up happening, that someone would prove that the Great Pyramid wasn't Khufu's doing. After all, I had a geologist boyfriend and geologists have been insisting for more than a century that all our calculations are way off. You know, the degree of erosion and all that."

"More arguments in my favour. Not only have we found Khufu's tomb. Not only have we found his mummy. Not only have we found among his grave goods the confession that he spent a fortune on clearing sand from the platform upon which the pyramids are constructed and on restoring their defects. Not only does he confide that the pyramids were already eroded during his reign. No, my dear. As a bonus, he informs us that 'Khafre, the son of my brother, will complete the restoration of the polish on the second pyramid.' Nobody ever suspected Khafre was Khufu's nephew. What is more, we have found a labyrinth of passages and an extremely ancient chamber with a set of mummies dating back much further than that of

Khufu himself. The preliminary estimate dates the twelve mummies to over 6,000 years ago. And that is not news? It astounds me. The news is that a large rock is hurtling towards Earth. I cannot fathom it, I simply cannot. On tomorrow morning's news programmes, instead of Khufu's sarcophagus appearing, we shall be watching the pretty face of... What was her name? Mary? That young Mexican lady who read the President's announcement. The whole world more wrapped up in a lump of rock than our own history. I am not surprised that Doctor McCallum has taken to his bed, half ill."

"We should away to bed as well. Maybe things'll look brighter in the morning."

"Yes, perhaps you are right, Doctor Howard."

They go back to the hotel, step into the lift and wait. When the lift does not react, they press the button marked 6 and go up to their rooms, a single for Doctor Shepard and adjoining rooms for the Howard siblings.

"I bid you both a good night."

"Good night, Doctor Shepard. Oh, before I forget: don't be alarmed if you hear me scream."

"Scream, my dear?"

"Yes, my brother massages my back before I go to sleep."

"A massage?"

"Yes, he's a grand masseuse, but a little rough sometimes. Anyway, whatever you hear, don't be alarmed, all right?"

Day 3

Sunday, 5 May 2030

"What the caterpillar calls the end, the rest of the world calls a butterfly."
Lao Tsu.

1

Houston
Local Time: 08.30

"While we can confirm that President Harry Grant is here, along with Benjamin Fischer, representative for the Secretary of Defence, and we do have confirmation that the Air Force has activated the Defcon 3 alert, the latest press release insists that the public should remain calm and continue with life as normal. They assure us that there is no cause for alarm. This is Louise Clarke at the Space Centre reporting for Channel 34."

Mecca
Local Time: 12.30

"It is impossible to say how many people have congregated around Mecca, attempting to enter the sacred precinct. I could not even venture an approximate figure. Millions of people are trying to access the holy site and many of us fear there may be another stampede. We cannot confirm the number of injured. What we can say is that over five hundred people have been evacuated by air or land and it seems some of them are in critical condition."

HORUS

New York
Live Debate, Channel 12
Local Time: 16.30

"We're not giving the numerical data the importance it deserves. We already know that rumour has it that the proportions of the vessel match those of Noah's Ark: one to six and one to ten. In other words, in a tripled version, we'd have a vessel measuring five units wide, three units high and thirty units long. Initial contact was established by the cargo spaceship *Antipodes* on May 3rd 2030, five three thirty. Exactly the same numbers. That can't be a coincidence!

But there's even more: in the Mayan long count calendar it would have been day 13.0.17.11.2. Between the date written in our calendar and the date written in the Mayan system, we have all the prime numbers and no non-prime numbers from zero to seventeen, precisely the limit set by the winal figure, which, as everyone knows, cannot exceed 17. That can't be a coincidence either. The dimensions of the object and the date of their visit have been deliberately chosen by an intelligence at least as developed as our own."

"If there is a crew on this vessel, I don't know what degree of intelligence they will have, but it has to be higher than yours, that's for sure. The calendars used on a planet are directly related to its rotational speed. Beings from another planet can't have taken that into account. For the love of God, let's be serious."

"You don't mean to tell me you think the fact that the numbers coincide is happenstance?"

"Coincide, coincidental, happenstance, that's right, you said it yourself."

"I thought this debate would be more intellectual, I really did."

HORUS

*Amsterdam
Local Time: 17.00*

"I'm standing in front of the Polyclinic in Fokkezeil Street in Banne, a residential area in the north of Amsterdam. All the signs indicate this is the residence of the hacker, or should I say information technician, who posted the video supposedly captured by the camera of mechanic Mike Gould, a member of the crew on the cargo spaceship *Antipodes*, on the web. According to this video, the extraterrestrial spacecraft approaching our planet contains coffin-shaped boxes with smaller receptacles inside them, numbering a total of 144,000. No church authority, either Catholic or Protestant, or any non-Christian religious body has wanted to comment on this figure, despite the obvious coincidence with the number who will be saved according to the Book of Revelation. As for the authenticity of the recording, the last Internet survey showed that around seventy per cent of respondents believed the video was genuine."

New Delhi
Local Time: 17.00

"Tragically, the number of drowned children continues to rise and now stands at eighty-two. The local authorities have spent several hours trying to control the crowds, especially the incessant parade of parents obsessed with the idea that their children should be in the sacred waters of the Ganges when the visitor purifies the earth with its arrival. They are convinced that the visitor's mission is to gather the souls of the pure and take them to a higher planet because ours is about to complete its life cycle, and they think the spaceship will travel the course of the Ganges to collect these pure souls. Conversely, they fear that everyone who is not chosen by the visitor will reincarnate on a planet far worse than Earth because, as we mentioned, it has reached the end of its life cycle and should therefore cease to be home to live organisms.

Meanwhile, devotees of the goddess Kali have been sacrificing the fifth child in their families and the authorities have been unable to enter the site, where the only access point is being guarded by heavily armed believers. Everything indicates that police will enter by force at any moment. In fact, there are more than a hundred officers on standby."

HORUS

San Francisco
Live Interview, Channel 23
Local Time: 12.30

"We're focusing on a lot of tiny details and we're not paying attention to one of the longest-running rumours flying around the Internet: the fact that the dimensions of the object are the same as Noah's ark. I think that's the key to the whole issue. What Noah did on a planetary scale, this vessel is going to repeat at a cosmic scale. It's travelling around to all the inhabited planets to pick up pairs of living beings. The difference is that they don't need adult animals now; they only need the nuclei of cells. The thousands of boxes on the vessel will be used to store DNA samples. This spaceship could hold samples of all living organisms from all the star systems which have had some sort of life form. I think the conclusion is obvious: Noah saved the earth's animals from a catastrophe at a planetary scale and this new ark from outer space is going to save us from a catastrophe on a galactic scale."

"Including us?"

"I hope so. After all, the rest of creation was made for us."

Padua
Local Time: 18.30

"We are coming to you from the modest church of the Madonna Addolorata al Torresino, where, according to several witnesses, the image of the Virgin Mary wept blood last night and in the early hours of this morning. The faithful have come from all the villages in the region to attend a religious ceremony and most of the congregation is out in the street because the church is packed to the rafters. Normally around forty or fifty people attend mass in this small church but I've been told that at five p.m. there were well over three hundred inside alone."

HORUS

Vatican City
Local Time: 18.30

"His Holiness Pope Benedict XIX remains in his private quarters, despite the fact that over two hours have passed since the first incidences occurred and thousands of people continue to arrive in the area surrounding Saint Peter's Square. This humble reporter cannot understand how His Holiness can possibly maintain his silence. Not even his spokespeople have given us the slightest indication of his thoughts, not a word. Oh, wait a moment... Hold on... We're getting something... Yes... Can you confirm that? Yes... The news is being confirmed... I can't hear very well... The Holy See has suffered... What? A heart attack. It appears he is being transferred to the Our Lady of the Sacred Heart hospital. Yes... Just a moment... Hold on! What is that noise? Who are you? You can't come in here... We'll keep you informed..."

Bonn
Live Interview, Channel 2
Local Time: 19.30

"As I said, I suspect it is not actually an extraterrestrial vessel. It's a natural object that is coming towards Earth. Last year the Apofis asteroid brushed past us. This year it's headed for full impact. They don't want us to know, so they've concocted this fairy tale about a peaceful vessel from outer space, which only wants to collect DNA samples. I think it's a white lie. And if I cause panic, I don't care. I'm not a politician, I don't have to lie to anyone."

2

Cairo
Local Time: 13.00

The restaurant has a good number of news channels available and the most prominent statement on all of them is the fact that the unidentified object is hurtling towards Earth at the incredible speed of three million kilometres per hour and, according to expert predictions, is due to arrive on Monday at 10 or 11 a.m. Greenwich Mean Time. A high proportion of the channels mention the discovery of Khufu's tomb, but they dispatch the subject in few words without giving it much importance. Even the local channels dedicate less time to it than might be expected and always far less than they spend on the intruder. Even the history channels refer to the visitor as a momentous event in the history of mankind while relegating the scrolls found in Khufu's subterranean mausoleum to a minor aside.

Ted Howard and Mathias Shepard are drinking a cinnamon-based Egyptian beverage while they wait for Nancy, who said half an hour ago, "I'll be right down."

"I would never have believed it," says Shepard. "The most important discovery since the Rosetta Stone and they only give it three sentences. We discover Khufu's tomb and we only capture the attention of a handful of experts."

"You know what," says Ted, "we should take matters into our own hands."

"I am not sure I follow you, Doctor Howard."

"Years ago I read *The Gods Themselves* by Isaac Asimov. A character manages to translate some very difficult inscriptions, Etruscan I think, and this guy congratulates him for translating a Latin text. Or something like that. The point is that this character says to himself, 'God, I've got to do something so crazy that even this gormless idiot learns it by heart.'"

"Are you suggesting we do something so outrageous that we become the protagonists on all the news channels?"

"But something linked to Ancient Egypt, to the pharaoh Khufu, to the scrolls found in his tomb, to the other burial chambers, to those unexpected 6,000-year-old mummies, so that there's no place left on earth that doesn't hear about these discoveries."

"And what do you propose we do, burn the pyramid? It is made of stone, it will not burn."

"What was I attempting to do before I came to Egypt?"

"You were trying to clone a mammoth if I recall correctly."

Doctor Howard leans forward and gestures for Doctor Shepard to do likewise so their heads are close together. In a low voice he says, "What if we clone Khufu?"

"Are you speaking in earnest?"

"Can you imagine, Doctor Shepard, the commotion it would cause when we present it to the world at a press conference to which we've invited the journalists with a promise of a great scoop but with no details of what it is?"

"My God!"

"Can you imagine the look on their faces when we say, 'Ladies and gentlemen, this child is the pharaoh Khufu.'"

"They would say we were completely mad. Nobody would believe a newborn baby could be Khufu."

"But the DNA test would prove that it is Khufu. That the child's DNA is the same as the DNA in Khufu's mummy. Remember what we talked about at the airport about tissue preservation? It's as if the mummies were inviting us to clone them, remember? Well, let's do just that."

"But, wait. It is one thing to clone a mammoth and quite another to clone a human being. Human rights must be respected."

"What if we claim that by cloning him, we are complying with his wishes. What if we say that mummification was done precisely for this purpose, to preserve the DNA of the dead so they could later be cloned?"

"It is an absurd idea if you consider for a moment. We can clone a body that is identical to Khufu, but we cannot clone who he was. We cannot replicate his memories therefore he would be a different person."

"We still don't know how to decipher all the information DNA contains, but we do know if it underwent any modifications during the organism's lifetime. You," Ted says, pointing a finger at Doctor Shepard, "suggested that Isis and Osiris were members of a more advanced extraterrestrial civilisation. Perhaps that civilisation knew how to extract a finer strand of DNA than we know how to extract. And that's why their descendants inherited the obsession with preserving some healthy tissue. But that's not the point right now. The point is not whether we're capable of resuscitating Khufu, personal memory included, of course we aren't. We're only talking about whether we will get everyone's attention by cloning his body or not."

"I need to assimilate the idea. Either way, we would have to take samples of Khufu's tissue in the utmost secrecy. And it would have to be done today. We start cataloguing everything we have found, down to the last splinter, first thing tomorrow morning. We would have started today, but nobody wants to deny McCallum the privilege."

"We're assuming he'll be on his feet tomorrow morning, I suppose?"

"Yes. And as soon as he has recovered the entire team will enter the hypogeum and there will be no way to lift a finger without it being recorded."

"Let's seize the chance while we can then. What's stopping you? Scruples? Fear? Worst-case scenario: the guards notice we've entered the excavation area. So what?"

"I do not know whether I have scruples, but I do know that I am not afraid. Tell me something, won't we need a woman to gestate the foetus?"

"You don't need to worry about that," says Nancy, who was sitting behind a pillar. "I might volunteer."

"But...!"

"Don't get cold feet now, little brother. From what I heard, it's your idea."

"What? How long have you been there?"

"A while. So the plan is clear. Now, let's enjoy a spot of lunch and as soon as it cools down a little we'll go and get the samples. Before something else comes up."

3

Space Monitoring Centre
Houston
Local Time: 21.30

"Well?"

"Confirmed. They'll be here tomorrow first thing."

"Any intelligible message?"

"None."

"Even I'm getting nervous," says the President. "Go and rest all of you. That's an order."

"What about you, sir?"

"Go and sleep, Fischer. I must have drunk twenty cups of coffee. I'm not in the least bit tired."

"I wouldn't be able to sleep either," says Mary.

"If you want, sit with me and tell me about Mexico."

"Mr President, forgive me but I don't understand what you're still doing here. With all due respect, shouldn't you go to Washington? Or to that mountain full of tunnels, to stay out of sight until all possible danger has passed?"

"Dear Mary, you're just like Fischer. You have no faith in hunches."

4

Cairo
Local Time: 23.30

"It's bloody freezing in the desert as soon as the sun goes down. You could've warned me and I'd have wrapped up a bit warmer," Ted grumbles to his sister.

"Just wait and see how hot it gets underground. It's better we're dressed like this."

"Your sister is right. We will be walking through very narrow passages; it's better to be a little on the chilly side now."

"Very narrow?"

"Yes. You don't suffer from claustrophobia I hope?"

"I don't think so. How narrow?"

"Extremely. In some stretches one must advance sideways and I barely fit: the walls brush my chest and back at the same time. A more ample man would be unable to pass."

"How many metres do you have to walk like that?"

"Perhaps it is best not to talk numbers. Distance can be deceptive inside. Careful with the slope, that's it, carefully does it. We enter here."

Doctor Shepard points at a crack between two rocks. It looks like a burrow.

"In there? What about the entrance we used this morning?"

"This morning we were on an official visit. The fewer people who see us, the better."

"I'm starting to regret coming on this adventure."

"What did you think the dig would be like? Did you imagine hostesses at the entrance, automatic doors, carpets, air conditioning? I'm afraid that archaeological digs continue to be as uncomfortable as they were in the nineteenth century. We are going to enter a very complex underground labyrinth, built on at least seven levels. If we were to take all the passages and put them in a line, they would stretch halfway around the earth. Losing one's nerves inside there is a death sentence, so please try to relax Doctor Howard."

"You're not making it easy."

"Banish it from your mind. Remember that I will be in front and I was the head of the team that drew the map of the parts we have unearthed. Moreover, we are not looters. We are legitimate researchers with the blessing of our university and the Egyptian government, which authorised the work following payment of a discrete compensation. So we are at liberty to enter with our lanterns lit. You have no idea what an advantage that gives us."

"Do you know what it's like to go through a tunnel without the lanterns?"

"Ah, the stories I could tell you… This way. Careful, duck down here. And don't worry, I know this part as well as my own home."

"That's good. What about when we reach the new part of the excavations?"

"I shall get my bearings."

"Are you sure we can't leave it until tomorrow?"

"Doctor Howard, at our luncheon you talked of nothing but Ancient Egypt, the scrolls and the value of the find, but in reality you wish to clone Khufu to rub it in Kasigi's face, do you not? You want the whole world to say, 'Doctor Kasigi's achievement has been surpassed: Doctor Howard has cloned Khufu, a pharaoh of the fourth dynasty, who died 2,500 years before Christ, from a sample extracted from his mummy.' Or am I mistaken?"

"No, you're not mistaken. I don't want trophies or cheques or applause. I want a photo of Kasigi's face when he finds out."

"Well, your reward lies within and tomorrow morning it will no longer be there. Look, we have to go down this well now. Are you with me?"

"Of course."

"Doctor Howard, perhaps you should stay out here," Shepard addresses Nancy.

"The role of macho protector of the flock doesn't suit you, Doctor Shepard."

"Very well. Stay close to me."

They descend into the well, which must be at least fifteen metres deep, clinging onto a rope ladder. One by one their feet find the bottom of the well, where the three of them barely fit side by side. The circular wall surrounding them has three openings in it.

"This way," says Doctor Shepard.

They crawl along a twenty-metre stretch before reaching a cave, where they see the mouths of three passages just large enough for an adult to crawl through.

"That way," he says. They drop to their knees again and shuffle along for thirty metres, stopping from time to time to lie down and stretch their legs. The trio reaches another cavern, where the roughness of the walls would make it appear like a natural grotto except for the fact there are inscriptions chiselled on one of the walls.

"They are orientation signs," says Doctor Shepard. "Follow me."

"It's like an ant's nest," says Ted.

"Yes. It turns out that all the burial complexes are connected to one another. It is like a city hidden beneath the sand."

After half an hour of moving through the labyrinth they reach the corridors leading to Khufu's burial site, which has three levels and a total of twelve chambers, the deepest of which contains the pharaoh's remains. For reasons hitherto unknown, the vertical line of this chamber is almost at the midpoint between the sphinx and the centre of Khafre's pyramid, the pharaoh for whom no mummy and treasure has ever been found.

The three doctors enter the last chamber. Measuring almost a hundred metres square, the room has beautiful decorations on all the walls. The wooden sarcophagus, almost six metres long, tarred and then painted mostly in yellow and blue, lies slightly off-centre to the right and further back from the side through which they entered. Inside the sarcophagus lies another and inside that yet another. The inner sarcophagus contains the mummy and has the same dimensions as its stone twin inside the King's Chamber of the Great Pyramid.

"Do we know why the sarcophagus is situated in such an unexpected spot just between Khafre and the sphinx?"

"No," replies Mathias Shepard, "but I suspect it's the geometric centre of the entire Giza complex."

"An excellent explanation, Doctor Shepard," says a voice behind them, a deep voice with a foreign accent. "I do not have a better one."

The three of them turn abruptly. Shocked to his very core, Ted exclaims, "Doctor Kasigi!"

With two bodyguards at his side, Doctor Kasigi approaches Ted. The tall bodyguards have shaved blond hair and are wearing black uniforms.

"That is correct. Everyone recognises me. Wherever I go, everyone who meets me knows my name. The consequences of fame. Is it the same for you, my dear Doctor Howard?"

"No, it's not the same for me. Nobody outside Scotland knows who I am."

"Outside Scotland? Don't you mean outside your department?"

"What have you lost in Egypt, Doctor Kasigi?"

Instead of answering, Kasigi walks in a semicircle around the trio, stopping next to Nancy.

"You are the only one who inspires a little respect. Your two companions, Doctor Howard, are nothing more than ingenuous trifles. I did not even bother to drug them like McCallum. You are the only one who caused me any doubts. But the idea of leaving the three of you trapped in here was so tempting, I could not resist."

"Trapped? Down here?"

"Do not despair. Once we have moved everything you will be free to go. At dawn we will begin work. We shall open an access tunnel large enough for a car to enter and then we shall take everything."

"Move everything? You shall have nothing to do with any moving," says Shepard. "The head of this dig is Doctor McCallum. Before moving anything, the entire find must be catalogued and when things are moved, it must be done according to protocol. Do you know how much destruction opening this tunnel of yours will cause?"

Kasigi and his henchmen let the professor speak before putting a pistol to his head. To Doctor Shepard's amazement, it is a Luger. Kasigi seems to read his mind.

"No, it is not a real Luger, it is a replica. You were saying who was in charge here?"

"You, Doctor Kasigi. You are in charge."

"Good. I am pleased to see you learn quickly. The move will be directed by me and in my own way. Perhaps you thought a British university would have the honour?"

"You want to take all this to Japan?"

"Take a closer look at my companions. What do they look like to you?"

"German?"

"Ja, mein Herr. My only loyalty is to the emperor and Yamamoto Takeshisama. However, at present I have the honour of working for the Berlin Museum. My German friends and I could not bear the idea of the Egyptian collection in the British Museum surpassing the one in Berlin. You British made many populations work hard for you: Afghans, Pakistanis, Arabs, Tunisians and especially the Indians, you came along and took everything down to the last rupee to fatten up your empire. Things have changed. Now you are the ones who work hard and, when you make a find, we come along and take it all away."

"We?"

"The Japanese and Germans. Working together like the old days. But this time there will be no mistakes. And one day..." Kasigi moves closer to Mathias Shepard and glares into his eyes. "One day, believe me, we will move the British Museum to Berlin. In its entirety!"

"But..."

"Silence! Not a word. Go down there."

They walk down some steps into a new labyrinth, narrower and darker than the previous one.

"Are you not excited, Doctor Shepard? We discovered these galleries today, while you were eating and discussing the possibility of cloning Khufu."

"Have you been watching us?" asks Ted.

"I have been watching you for years, Doctor Howard. After all, the work which enabled me to clone the mammoth is almost all yours. I am grateful to you, particularly for the chromosomic reintegration in acid."

"That method didn't work!"

"Yes, that is what your assistants had you believe."

The curious party reaches a chamber which contains seventy-two sarcophagi arranged in a six-by-twelve matrix. They move through it, walk through a narrow corridor for nearly thirty metres, descend another level and reach a small empty room.

"Give me your torches. You have meddled in places you should not have done, so you will have to stay here temporarily. Do not be overly concerned, you will only be here a night or two. Then we shall take you to a more comfortable place. And once we have moved everything, which may take less than three months, you can go home."

Kasigi reaches the door and turns.

"Do not think I am as bad as I seem at this instant. As proof of my camaraderie, Doctor Howard, I will personally ensure that your idea of cloning Khufu comes to fruition. And as proof of my friendship towards you two, if you visit the Berlin Museum, please tell them you are my guests at the ticket booth."

The three doctors hear the unmistakeable sound of large stones being dragged. They are left in utter darkness and the most profound silence almost fifty metres underground.

Day 4

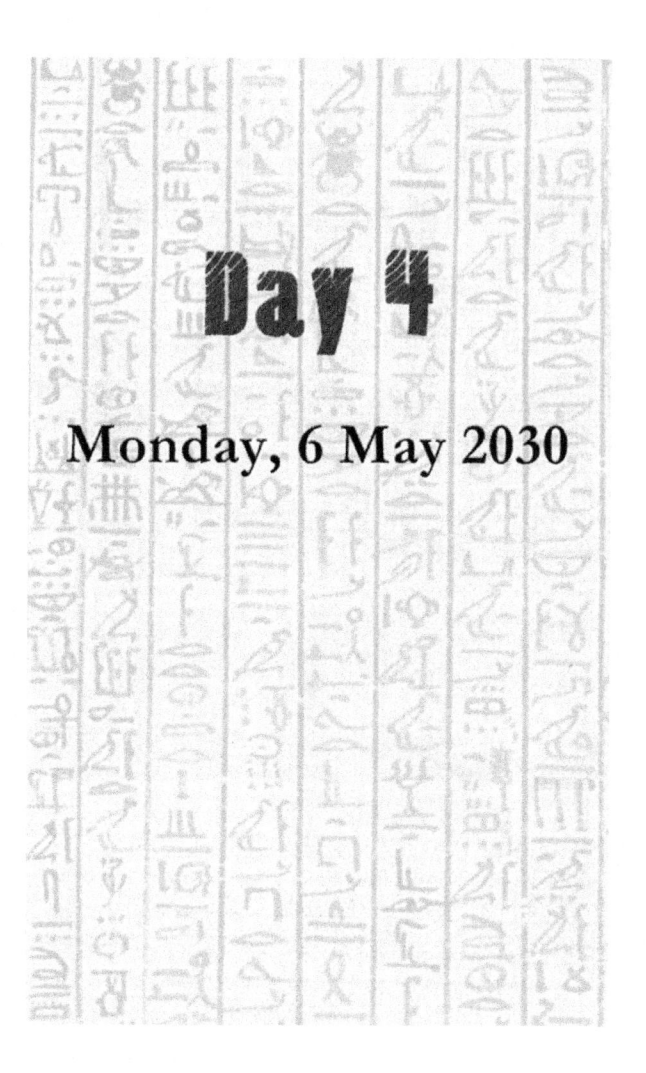

Monday, 6 May 2030

"Man is an experiment... Time will show whether they were worth the trouble."

Mark Twain.

HORUS

1

Space Monitoring Centre
Houston
Local Time: 04.30

The situation is so tense that nobody feels tired, despite not having slept well since Thursday. The members of the Space Monitoring team and the presidential entourage have invaded the facilities of the Earth Monitoring department. Only the departmental specialists are seated, observing their monitors. The others are standing about, nervously biting their crutch of preference: nails, toothpicks, pencils.

"They've entered the atmosphere," says John Hepburn, who is looking at a terminal receiving a direct signal from Moscow. "It's still surrounded by an almost perfectly spherical membrane, 550 metres in diameter."

Three generals stand next to the President, ready to take orders.

"It's come in over Siberia, direction 270. Altitude: a hundred thousand feet. Approximate speed: fifteen thousand knots. Mach 22."

"Did you say Mach 22? That's nigh on impossible," says General Simmons.

"It's leaving a wind wake," says Hepburn.

"Even at a hundred thousand feet?"

"That is unconfirmed data. Wait! It's braking! It's dropped to Mach 4 over…"

"The Tunguska River," says Henry Lance, looking at four television signals and two interactive maps. "It's rotated north and is flying over the Podkamennaya Tunguska River."

"What's there?" asks the President.

"Nothing that I know of," replies Lance.

"An explosion. A ten-megaton explosion happened there in 1908," says General Bowers.

"What's that got to do with anything?"

"It's accelerating again. Mach 7. Oh my God! Mach 20 and accelerating... It's headed for Moscow. It'll be there in under 10 minutes," Lance concludes.

"Sir!" shouts Matt Lewis, who is responsible for attending to alpha-level messages. "Message from the presidency of Moscow. Their air defence systems are down. Nothing is working."

"Oh Lord," says the President. "Raise the alert to Defcon 4."

"Yes, sir," says General Brown, immediately starting to transmit orders through his own terminals.

"It'll reach Moscow in three minutes... two... one... It's passed Moscow. It's still flying at eighty thousand feet. Mach 20. Direction: Berlin," says Lance.

"Sir, Moscow's systems are fully operative again," says Lewis.

"Direction: Berlin. It will get there in a few minutes," Lance continues.

Eight minutes pass.

"Sir, nothing's working in Berlin. Total blackout. No, wait, that's not it. It's only the defence systems. The whole system's down," says Lewis.

"It's passed Berlin. It's flying over French territory, the Bay of Biscay," Lance comments.

"Berlin operative."

Everyone wants to talk at once, reporting what each of them sees on their screens.

"A hundred thousand feet over the Atlantic. Mach 20. Direction..."

"Washington," says Fischer. "After Moscow and Berlin, it must be headed to Washington."

"No, sir," says Hepburn. "It's not Washington. Wait a second... Confirmed. Direction: Houston."

"Houston? It's coming here?"

"It certainly looks that way, sir."

"What is it looking for?"

"Scramble the F28s in Delaware," says Harry Grant. "Without opening fire. Just get them to take a look and report back."

"Yes, sir," replies General Brown, who quickly makes another call on one of his private channels. "Sir, I'm afraid our fighter jets aren't operative. They can't take off. The defence systems aren't responding. We're at their mercy."

"They'll need a little over fifteen minutes to cross the Atlantic."

The minutes tick slowly by with little comment from

anyone.

"Object approaching. Four minutes... three... two... one... It's stopped directly above us."

The assembled military and non-military staff disperse, walking out onto the balconies, craning their necks out of windows or even venturing outside.

A grey balloon is descending. It looks like a toy balloon, a balloon that a child has let go of. But that is because it is still over ten thousand feet above them. It continues to descend. The optical illusion of it being a child's toy vanishes. It is a gigantic spherical object which continues to descend over the runways until its underbelly appears within arm's reach. The Pentagon would fit inside it with plenty of room to spare. It seems to have a living membrane, similar to the skin of an amphibian, furrowed with hundreds of capillaries. The skin turns transparent, it opens and separates. Only the upper half remains, like a dome. Two vessels come into view: the unidentified object, four hundred metres of storm cloud grey, and below it, attached by fine wires that are barely visible, the *Antipodes*, with the centrifuges turned off and the paint on the hull scorched and flaking.

The wires lengthen. While the extraterrestrial vessel remains static, the cargo spaceship *Antipodes* is lowered to the ground. The landing gear activates and it touches down gently. All the doors open and the cargo vessel crew walk out.

"They've brought us home," says Mike Gould. "How did they know where we're from?"

"They'll have tracked the origin of the signals," says Benson. "Welcome back."

"Welcome home," repeats the President. "I'm glad you're safe."

"Captain Tanner, it's good to see you," says Fischer, extending his hand.

"I'm sorry I called you big mouth."

"Don't worry, I've been called worse."

The wires are being retracted.

"What about our deal? I guess you're gonna tell me I haven't done my part."

"No, you didn't. But I should think you'll earn a good wad of dough."

"Are you gonna tell me how?"

The wires have disappeared. The vast machine starts to rise.

"I'm going to introduce you to Mary Sanchez. She's a journalist who became an overnight sensation. And you're the protagonist of a highly original story, so all the major newspapers are going to be bidding on you, not to mention the TV stations."

The membrane seems to be absorbed into the rectangular spacecraft. It heads southeast, this time without the spherical membrane around it.

Everyone returns to the Earth Monitoring room.

"Where's it going now?" asks the President.

"I don't know what to tell you, sir. It's not headed for a particular city. It's crossing the Gulf of Mexico towards the Yucatan Peninsula. It's headed for... Chichen Itza," says Hepburn.

"The Mayan pyramid?"

"It would seem so, sir."

"What on earth is it looking for? Hooper, surprise us with one of your ideas. It seems our friend is looking for something. Do you have any idea what it might be?"

"I don't think it's looking for something, sir. I think it's looking for someone."

2

Cairo
Local Time: 02.00

"Is there any way out of here?" asks Ted.

"I don't think so. This corridor to the right is only five or six metres long and then you reach a type of mud wall. And they've moved a stone to block the other passage, about twenty metres from this door. The best thing is to stay as we are, sitting on the ground. We should try to get some sleep," reasons Nancy.

"I can't sleep with all these mummies lying around me."

"They won't hurt you, believe me. Best get some sleep, the night will pass quicker."

"It's two o'clock and it feels like I've been here a month."

"Go to sleep for a while. When we're more rested, we'll find a way out."

3

Space Monitoring Centre
Houston
Local Time: 06.30

"It's over Chichen Itza. It's hovering over the pyramid." Hepburn continues his running commentary on the intruder's journey.

"I've got a signal from the local TV stations. The Mexican air force can't intervene: their equipment isn't responding. The transmitters and the power networks are working though. They say it's firing rays at the pyramid," says Lewis.

"Rays?"

"I'm connecting to the transmitter."

The monitors show a large expanse of grass with the pyramid in the background and a large shadow covering it completely from above. Few people have chosen this place to gather, but it seems they have got it right. From the large dark object, green, blue and red rays shoot out and pass through the ground, creating a lattice of light.

"Is it scanning the subsoil?" asks Colonel Benson.

"Something like that," says Hooper.

"We've got live audio," says Lewis.

"The rays of light let the visitor see underground, like an X-ray. There are hundreds of tunnels down there. It appears the red rays detect them and then the green rays search the interior of each tunnel. It's like a great subterranean city under there. You get the sense that it's exploring, searching for something. The lights have gone. They've turned off all the lights. It's rising. It's moving away at a tremendous speed, you can hardly see it now. I don't know what it was looking for, but whatever it was they haven't found it here."

"New direction. Calibrating. Initial direction 095. It's over the Atlantic now. Mach 1. Wait. The echo is getting bigger. It must be forming a new protective sphere. Yes, it's gaining altitude and accelerating. Sixty thousand feet. Mach 4. Mach 15. Adjusting direction..." Lance trails off.

"To where?" demands the President.

"Cairo, Egypt, sir. According to my calculations, it'll get there at 07.00 hours. There it will be... 12.00 hours. Midday."

4

Cairo
Local Time: 12.00

"Did you see that?" asks Nancy.

"It must be an optical illusion," says Doctor Shepard.

"It's a red light," says Ted.

"We have been trapped in here for almost twelve hours. Our eyes are imagining things. Our eyes are... Ahh!" Doctor Shepard shields his eyes as the light shines directly on them.

"What the hell is that?" says Ted.

"It appears to be a laser. It seems to be coming from the upper floors," says Doctor Shepard.

"Watch out. That green light's coming now," Nancy warns.

5

Space Monitoring Centre
Houston
Local Time: 07.00

"It's stopped over the Giza plateau. It's scanning the subsoil, like it did in Chichen Itza. I've got a very poor visual. A local commentator is saying that he can see the network of tunnels, as though the ground were transparent. I've got live audio," says Lewis.

"People are hiding. They're scared out of their wits. The lights from this huge machine are making the underground chambers visible. We can see the passages, the sacred rooms, the burial chambers and even the bodies of the pharaohs themselves."

6

Cairo
Local Time: 12.10

The chamber in which Mathias Shepard and the Howard siblings have spent the night is inundated with green light, turning their faces and clothes a sickly shade. The ground beneath them has turned semi-transparent, revealing more levels below them. In the depths of the subterranean network, five or six levels below, they see a perfectly square chamber containing two large sarcophagi, which appear to be made of metal.

"Can you see that?" asks Ted.

"Yes, we see it, but we don't understand what it is," replies Nancy.

Silently, without breaking walls, without raising dust, a vertical tunnel forms above the chamber containing the two metal coffins. They know the tunnel reaches the surface because sunlight appears, albeit a tenuous light, as if it were dusk.

"That can't be right. It's midday. It must have clouded over," says Doctor Shepard.

"No, it's not cloudy. Some kind of object is casting a shadow, like the belly of a plane," Nancy explains.

The lead-coloured sarcophagi have disappeared from sight, replaced by two translucent bubbles. It seems the sarcophagi are inside them. They start to rise. Next to Mathias Shepard, illuminated in green, three more bubbles form. Each is just large enough to fit a person inside.

7

Space Monitoring Centre
Houston
Local Time: 07.15

"Don't ask me how it did that. That machine has bored a tunnel nearly ten metres in diameter. Or a chimney, call it what you want. With no drills, no dust. The sand just vanished," says Captain Tanner.

"We can see that," responds Patch.

"I can see it but I don't believe it," Crude adds.

"My dad should be here to see this," says Drill.

"Congratulations, Tanner: I reckon you'll be able to ask whatever you want for this exclusive," says Colonel Benson.

"I can't even think about money right now."

"Look! Two bubbles are coming out of the tunnel. They're carrying two... two..." exclaims Hooper.

"Two sarcophagi! But they're metal! Guys, I want all of this recorded," orders the President.

"They've gone inside the vessel. It looks like they've passed through the wall." Colonel Benson is incredulous.

"Look! Three more bubbles! They've got people inside!" says Hooper.

"I've got audio from the Egyptian commentator," says Lewis.

"It's hard to make them out. The facial recognition program is at max power. Wait... One of the bubbles is on the ground. It's opening. It's vanished. That's incredible, there's no bubble now. I need confirmation. Yes, it's Shepard, Doctor Mathias Shepard. He's fallen to the ground. The medics are attending him. The other two spheres are ascending towards the dark machine, which hasn't moved an inch. The facial recognition program has finished. Yes... I'm on air... I'm receiving data... Yes, they're confirming that it's brother and sister Ted and Nancy Howard. They've been taken inside the spaceship. It's rising, it's leaving. My God, it's leaving with two people inside. It's taken them away."

"Ten thousand feet. Twenty thousand. It's formed a new protective balloon. Mach 15... Mach 20... It's gone past the atmosphere. It's left Earth. It's left Earth and taken two people with it, sir," comments Lance.

"Yeah, I heard," says the President.

"It's moving away from Earth at great speed and accelerating, sir."

∨⊖≡⊕

HORUS

Place: **Unknown**
Date: **Spring**
Local Time: **Midday**

They are flying over a wooded area with a large river to the right. Wood and straw huts are visible. People are on the ground pointing up at the flying house that blocks the sun. The large flying house descends. It leaves Ted and Nancy Howard on the ground. There is a stone construction behind them. Two large dark metal sarcophagi are being lowered underground through a tunnel. They reach a square chamber deep beneath the surface. The tunnel closes by itself. The flying house leaves.

The local people, short and thin with very dark skin are lying face down on the ground, trembling with fear. One of the little men, dressed in something that looks like a tiger skin, approaches them. It is evident that he is afraid too, but he approaches. He is accompanied by a girl holding his hand. In the other hand he is holding a stone knife.

The man positions the girl at the feet of the new arrivals. He holds her by the neck, raises the knife and prepares to slit her throat.

"Nooooo!" yells Ted.

The man drops the knife and falls to the ground. He is so frightened he looks like he is about to vomit.

Ted observes the multitude. They lift their heads and

look at the newcomers with a mixture of fear and curiosity. Ted gestures for the girl to go back to her people. A woman runs to embrace her.

"Nancy, tell me I'm dreaming."

"I don't think you are."

"So what do we do now?"

"No idea. We'll think of something."

A Note of Thanks

Thanks for reading Horus. I hope you liked it and that you spend a few days discussing it with friends, finding the best interpretation of the final chapter, and that you remember it each time you see a photo of the pyramids.

Thanks and warm regards.

One Last Thing

With reason or without, I have spent many years thinking that my novels might be liked by the many fans of science fiction in both the United Kingdom and America. So for a long time I have been thinking of finding a person to translate them from Spanish into English. But, although I thought about it, I didn't actually lift a finger to find that person. Partly because a book and a child have something in common: you don't entrust them to just anyone.

Suddenly, one afternoon in October 2015, I don't know why, but I turned on my computer and told Google to search for translators. Three minutes later, Sarah Marshall appeared on my screen. And when I saw her profile, I knew I could trust her.

Thanks very much, Sarah: this book wouldn't exist without you.

MANUEL SANTOS VARELA

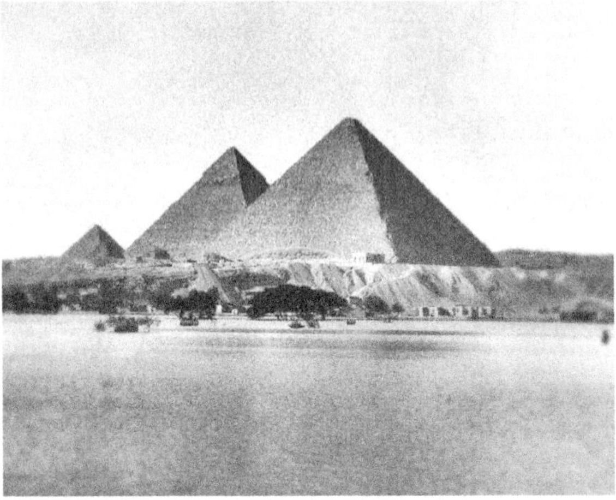

Manuel Santos Varela is a Spanish writer
born in Zaragoza in 1962.
An inveterate reader (novels, plays, brochures, comics,
poetry, encyclopaedias, film credits, T-shirt slogans,
graffiti, ancient inscriptions, etc.),
Santos Varela has been unable to resist the temptation to write.
It could be stated that he writes science fiction,
but he has no aversion to other genres;
in fact, what he likes best is mixing them up.
After graduating with an engineering degree in 1985,
he has been teaching since 1988.
Married with children, he cultivates the fine art of squeezing
as much as he can into each 24-hour period.
For more information, please visit www.about.me/thewriterinhislabyrinth

Born in 1972, Sarah Marshall grew up in Somerset, England
and has a combined honours degree in History
and English Literature from Anglia Polytechnic University.
Having worked in both private and public organisations
in the UK and as an English teacher to foreign students,
she has lived in or around Barcelona, Spain since 2004.
She has been translating from Spanish to English since 2007
and from Catalan to English since 2010.
While Sarah will turn her hand to many types of translation,
including textbooks, non-fiction and cultural texts, her lifelong passion
for words and reading has naturally led to a preference for literature.
With over twenty published translations of children's books,
she also enjoys the challenge of translating fiction for adults.
Sarah lives in a small village near Barcelona with her Catalan partner
and their two daughters.
For more information, please visit www.simplewords.es.

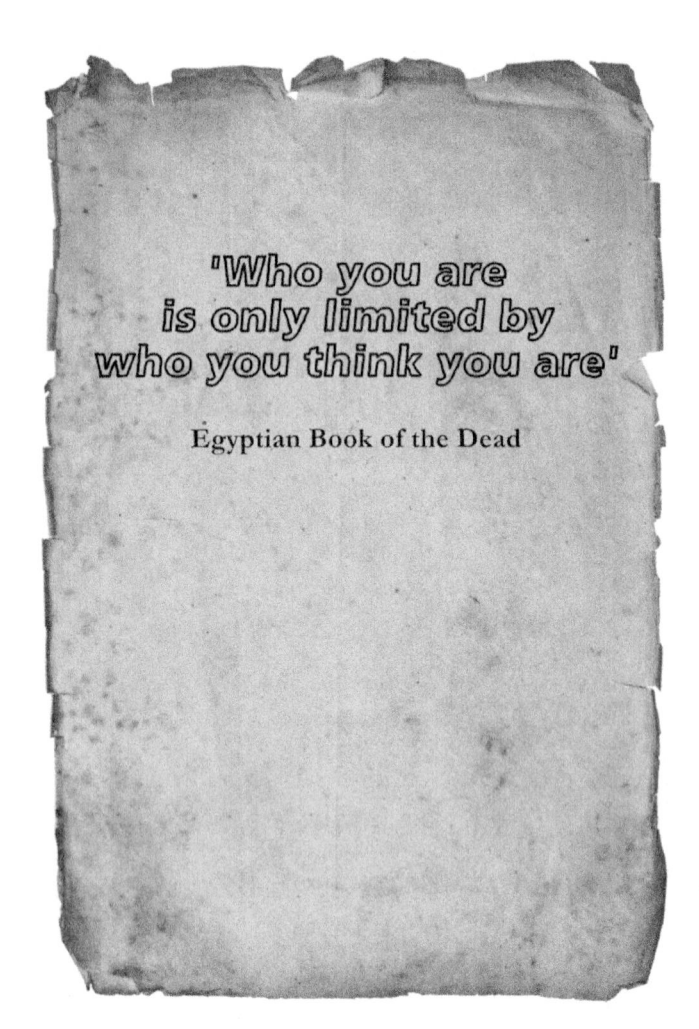

'Who you are
is only limited by
who you think you are'

Egyptian Book of the Dead

Printed in Great Britain
by Amazon